P9-CRU-185

MIDWIVES ON-CALL

Welcome to Melbourne Victoria Hospital—
and to the exceptional midwives
who make up the Melbourne Maternity Unit!

These midwives in a million work miracles
on a daily basis, delivering tiny bundles of joy
into the arms of their brand-new mums!

Amidst the drama and emotion of babies
arriving at all hours of the day and night, when
the shifts are over, somehow there's still time
for some sizzling out-of-hours romance...

Whilst these caring professionals might come
face-to-face with a whole lot of love in their
line of work, now it's their turn to find
a happy-ever-after of their own!

Midwives On-Call

Midwives, mothers and babies—
lives changing for ever...!

Dear Reader,

I was thrilled to be a part of the ***Midwives On-Call*** series, and to work alongside some of my favourite authors.

We all have secrets, or sides to ourselves that we might not reveal, and that really is the case with my heroine, Isla—she is outwardly strong, with a demanding job and an exciting social life, but there is a side to her that she lets no one see. I knew it would take a very special hero to discover the *real* Isla, behind the rather glamorous façade. Alessi is all that and more.

I hope you enjoy Isla and Alessi's story.

Happy reading!

Carol x

JUST ONE NIGHT?

BY
CAROL MARINELLI

First published in Great Britain 2015
by Mills & Boon, an imprint of Harlequin (UK) Limited,
Large Print edition 2015
Eton House, 18-24 Paradise Road,
Richmond, Surrey, TW9 1SR

Special thanks and acknowledgement are given to Carol Marinelli for her contribution to the *Midwives On-Call* series

ISBN: 978-0-263-25504-1

Harlequin (UK) Limited's policy is to use papers that are natural, renewable and recyclable products and made from wood grown in sustainable forests. The logging and manufacturing processes conform to the legal environmental regulations of the country of origin.

Printed and bound in Great Britain
by CPI Antony Rowe, Chippenham, Wiltshire

Carol Marinelli recently filled in a form where she was asked for her job title and was thrilled, after all these years, to be able to put down her answer as 'writer'. Then it asked what Carol did for relaxation. After chewing her pen for a moment Carol put down the truth—'writing'. The third question asked: 'What are your hobbies?' Well, not wanting to look obsessed or, worse still, boring, she crossed the fingers on her free hand and answered 'swimming and tennis'. But, given that the chlorine in the pool does terrible things to her highlights, and the closest she's got to a tennis racket in the last couple of years is watching the Australian Open, I'm sure you can guess the real answer!

Books by Carol Marinelli

Baby Twins to Bind Them
Unwrapping Her Italian Doc
Playing the Playboy's Sweetheart
200 Harley Street: Surgeon in a Tux
Tempted by Dr Morales
The Accidental Romeo
Secrets of a Career Girl
Dr Dark and Far Too Delicious

Visit the author profile page at millsandboon.co.uk for more titles

MIDWIVES ON-CALL

Midwives, mothers and babies—
lives changing for ever…!

Enter the magical world of the Melbourne Maternity Unit and the exceptional midwives there, delivering tiny bundles of joy on a daily basis. Now it's time to find a happy-ever-after of their own…

Just One Night? by Carol Marinelli
Gorgeous Greek doctor Alessi Manos is determined to charm the beautiful yet frosty Isla Delamere… but can he melt this ice queen's heart?

Meant-To-Be Family by Marion Lennox
When Dr Oliver Evans's estranged wife, Emily, crashes back into his life, old passions are re-ignited. But brilliant Dr Evans is in for a surprise… Emily has two foster-children!

Always the Midwife by Alison Roberts
Midwife Sophia Toulson and hard-working paramedic Aiden Harrison share an explosive attraction…but will they overcome their tragic pasts and take a chance on love?

Midwife's Baby Bump by Susanne Hampton
Hot-shot surgeon Tristan Hamilton's passionate night with pretty student midwife Flick has unexpected consequences!

Midwife…to Mum! by Sue MacKay
Free-spirited locum midwife Ally Parker meets top GP and gorgeous single dad Flynn Reynolds. Is she finally ready to settle down with a family of her own?

His Best Friend's Baby by Susan Carlisle
When beautiful redhead Phoebe Taylor turns up on ex-army medic Ryan Matthews's doorstep there's only one thing keeping them apart: she's his best friend's widow…and eight months pregnant!

Unlocking Her Surgeon's Heart by Fiona Lowe
Brooding city surgeon Noah Jackson meets compassionate Outback midwife Lilia Cartwright. Could Lilia be the key to Noah's locked-away heart?

Her Playboy's Secret by Tina Beckett
Renowned English obstetrician Darcie Green might think playboy Lucas Elliot is nothing but trouble— but is there more to this gorgeous doc than meets the eye?

Experience heartwarming emotion and pulse-racing drama in *Midwives On-Call*
this sensational eight-book continuity from Mills & Boon Medical Romance

PROLOGUE

'ISLA...' THE PANIC and fear was evident in Cathy's voice. 'What are all those alarms?'

'They're truly nothing to worry about,' Isla said, glancing over to the anaesthetist and pleased to see that he was changing the alarm settings so as to cause minimal distress to Cathy.

'Was it about the baby?'

Isla shook her head. 'It was just letting the anaesthetist know that your blood pressure is a little bit low but we expect that when you've been given an epidural.'

Isla sat on a stool at the head of the theatre table and did her best to reassure a very anxious Cathy as her husband, Dan, got changed to come into Theatre and be there for his wife.

'It's not the baby that's making all the alarms go off?' Cathy checked again.

'No, everything looks fine with the baby.'

'I'm so scared, Isla.'

'I know that you are,' Isla said as she stroked Cathy's cheek. 'But everything is going perfectly.'

This Caesarean section *had* to go perfectly.

Isla, head nurse at the Melbourne Maternity Unit at the Victoria Hospital, or MMU, as it was more regularly known, had been there for Dan and Cathy during some particularly difficult times. There was little more emotional or more difficult in Isla's work than delivering a stillborn baby and she had been there twice for Cathy and Dan at such a time. As hard as it was, there was a certain privilege to being there, too—making a gut-wrenching time somehow beautiful, making the birth and the limited time with their baby poignant in a way that the family might only appreciate later.

Cathy and Dan's journey to parenthood had

been hellish. They had undergone several rounds of IVF, had suffered through four miscarriages and there had been two stillbirths which Isla had delivered.

Now, late afternoon on Valentine's Day, their desperately wanted baby was about to be born.

Cathy had initially been booked in next Thursday for a planned Caesarean section at thirty-seven weeks gestation. However, she had rung the MMU two hours ago to say that she thought she was going into labour and had been told to come straight in.

Cathy had delivered her other babies naturally. Even though the labours had often been long and difficult with a stillborn, it was considered better for the mother to deliver that way.

As head of midwifery, Isla's job was supposedly nine to five, only she had long since found out that babies ran to their own schedules.

This evening she'd had a budget meeting scheduled which, on the news of Cathy's arrival, Isla had excused herself from. As well as that, she'd had drinks scheduled at the Rooftop Garden Bar to welcome Alessandro Manos, a neonatologist who was due to start at the Victoria on Monday.

For now it could all simply wait.

There was no way that Isla would miss this birth.

At twenty-eight years of age Isla was young for such a senior position and a lot of people had at first assumed that Isla had got the job simply because her father, Charles Delamere, was the CEO of the Victoria.

They'd soon found out otherwise.

Yes, outside the hospital Isla and her sister Isabel, the obstetrician who was operating on Cathy this evening, were very well known thanks to their prominent family. Glamorous, gorgeous and blonde, the press followed the sisters' busy lives with interest. There were many functions they were expected to attend and the two women shared a luxurious penthouse and dressed in the latest designer clothes and regularly stepped onto the red carpet.

That was all work to Isla.

The MMU was her passion, though—here she was herself.

She sat now dressed in scrubs, her long blonde hair tucked beneath a pink theatre cap, her full lips hidden behind a mask, and no one cared in the theatre that she was Isla Delamere, Melbourne socialite, apparently dating Rupert, whom she had gone to school with and who was now a famous Hollywood actor.

To everyone here she was simply Isla—strict, fair and loyal. She expected the same focus and attention from her staff that she gave to the patients, and she generally got it. Some thought her cool and aloof but the mothers generally seemed to appreciate her calm professionalism.

'Here's Dan.' Isla smiled as Dan nervously made his way over. He really was an amazing man and had been an incredible support to his wife through the dark times. His tears had been shed in private, he had told Isla, well away from his shocked wife. Many had said he should share the depths of his grief with Cathy but Isla understood why he chose not to.

Sometimes staying strong meant holding back.

'Dan, I'm sure that something is wrong...' Cathy said.

Dan glanced over at Isla, who gave him a small, reassuring shake of the head as her eyes told him that everything was fine.

'Everything is going well, Cathy,' Dan said. 'You're doing an amazing job, so just try and relax...'

'I can feel something,' Cathy said in a panicked voice, and Isla stepped in.

'Do you remember that I said you would feel some tugging?' Isla reminded her.

'Cathy!' Isabel's voice alerted Isla. 'Your baby is nearly out—look up at the screen...'

Isla looked up to the green sheets that had been placed so that Cathy could not see the surgery going on on the other side. 'Your baby is out,' Isabel said, 'and looks amazing…'

'There's no crying,' Cathy said.

'Just wait, Cathy,' Dan said, his voice reassuring his wife, though the poor man must be terrified.

Even Isla, who was very used to the frequent delay between birth and tears, found that she was holding her breath, though Cathy could never have guessed her midwife's nerves—Isla hid her emotions extremely well.

And not just from the staff and patients.

'Cathy!' Isla said. 'Look!'

There he was.

Isabel was holding up a beautiful baby boy with a mass of dark, spiky hair. His mouth opened wide and he let out the most ear-piercing scream, absolutely furious to be woken from a lovely sleep, to be born, of all things!

'He's beautiful,' Dan said. 'Cathy, look how beautiful he is. You did so well, I'm so proud of you.'

The baby was whisked away for a brief check and Isla made her way over as Isabel continued with the surgery.

He really was perfect.

Four weeks early, he was still a nice size and very alert. The paediatrician was happy with him and the theatre midwife wrapped him in a pale cream blanket and popped on a small hat. He would be more thoroughly checked later but that visit to the parents, if well enough, came first.

Isla took the little baby, all warm and crying, into her arms and she felt a huge gush of emotion. She had known that this birth would be emotional, but the feeling of finally being able to hand this gorgeous couple a healthy baby was a special moment indeed.

She held the baby so that Cathy could turn her head and give him a kiss and then Isla placed him on Cathy's chest as Dan put his arms around his little family.

Isla said nothing. They deserved this time to

themselves and she did all she could to make this time as private as a theatre could allow it to be. She stood watching as they met their son. Dan properly broke down and cried in front of his wife for the first time.

'I can't believe I'm finally a mum…' Cathy said, and then her eyes lifted and met Isla's. 'I mean…'

When Isla spoke, she was well aware of the conflicting feelings that Cathy might have.

'You've been a mum for a very long time,' Isla said, gently referring to their difficult journey. 'Now you get the reward.'

Isla's time with Cathy and Dan didn't finish there, though. After Cathy had been sutured and Recovery was happy with her status, Isla saw them back to the ward. Cathy simply could not stop looking at her baby and Dan was immensely proud of both his wife and son.

They had made it to parenthood.

Before Cathy was discharged Isla would have a long talk with her. Often with long-awaited babies depression followed. It was a very confusing time for the new mother—often she felt guilty as everyone around her was telling her how happy she must be, how perfect things were. In fact, exhaustion, grief over previous pregnancies, failure to live up to the standards they had set themselves could cause a crushing depression in the postnatal period. Isla would speak with both Dan and Cathy about it before the family went home.

But not tonight.

For now it really was about celebrating this wonderful new life.

'I'm going to have a glass of champagne for you tonight,' Isla said as she left them to enjoy this special time.

She said goodbye to the staff on the ward then headed around to the changing room.

She'd forgotten her dress, Isla realised as soon as she opened her locker. She could picture it hanging on her bedroom door and hadn't remembered to grab it when she'd dashed for work that morning.

She glanced at the time and realised she would be horribly late if she went home to change. She knew that she really ought to go straight there as there weren't many people able to make it, given that it was Valentine's Day. Alessandro had apparently been doing a run of nights in his previous job and had booked to go away for the weekend with his girlfriend before he started his new role.

Isla rummaged through her locker to see if there was an outfit that she could somehow cobble together. She didn't have much luck! There was a pair of denim shorts that she had intended to wear with runners. Isla had actually meant to start walking during her lunch break but, of course, it had never happened. She could hardly turn up at the Rooftop Bar in shorts and the skimpy T-shirt and runners that she had in her locker, but then she saw a pair of cream wedged espadrilles that she had lent to a colleague and which had been returned.

Isla tried it all on but the sandals pushed her outfit from far too casual to far too tarty.

Oh, well, it would have to do. She was more than used to turning heads. She didn't even question if there was a dress code that needed to be adhered to. Isla didn't have to worry about such things—it was one of the perks of being a Delamere girl. You were welcome everywhere and dress codes simply didn't apply.

She ran a comb through her long blonde hair and added a quick dash of lip gloss and some blusher before racing out of the maternity unit and hailing a taxi. As she sat in the back seat she realised that she was slightly out of breath—she hadn't yet come down from the wonderful birth she had just witnessed.

Elated.

That was how she felt as she climbed the stairs and then stepped into the Rooftop Bar.

And that was how she looked when Alessi first

saw her. Tall, blonde and with endless brown legs, she walked into the bar with absolute confidence. She looked vaguely familiar, he thought, though he couldn't place her. At first he didn't even know if she was a part of the small party that was gathered.

He knew, though, that, whoever she was, he would be making an effort to speak with her tonight. He watched as she gave a small wave and made her way over and he found out her name as the group greeted her.

'Isla!'

So *this* was Isla.

Alessi knew who she was then. Not just that she was head midwife at The Victoria. Not just that she must be Charles Delamere's younger daughter, which would explain why she was in such a high-up role at such a young age. No, it was more than that. Though he could not remember her from all those years ago, he knew the name—they had attended the same school.

'I'm sorry that I'm so late.' Isla smiled.

'How did it go?' Emily, one of the midwives, asked, referring to Cathy's delivery.

'It was completely amazing,' Isla said. 'I'm so lucky to have been there.'

'And I'm so jealous that you were!' Emily teased, and then made the introductions. 'Isla, this is Alessandro Manos, the new neonatologist.'

Isla only properly saw him then and as she turned her slight breathlessness increased.

He was seriously gorgeous with black, tousled curly hair and he was very unshaven. The moment she first met his black eyes all Isla could think was that she wished Rupert were here tonight.

Isla and Rupert were seemingly the golden couple. They had been together since school, where Isla had been head girl and Rupert had been head of the debating team. One night they had gone to a party and it had been there, after a very awkward kiss, that Rupert had confessed to her that he was gay.

Rupert had no idea how his parents would take the news and he was also upset at some of the rumours that were going around the school.

Isla had covered for him then and she still did to this very day.

Rupert's career had progressed over the years and his agent had strongly advised him that the roles that were being offered would be far harder to come by if the world knew the truth. He was nothing more than a wonderful friend who, in recent years, had questioned why Isla chose to keep up the ruse that they were going out.

It suited Isla, too.

Despite her apparent confidence, despite her ease in social situations, despite the questions raised by magazines about her morals, because she put up with Rupert's supposed unfaithfulness after all, no one had ever come close to the truth—Isla was a virgin.

Her entire sexual history could be written on the back of a postage stamp. She'd had one schoolgirl kiss with Rupert that hadn't gone well at all. Now she'd had several more practised kisses with Rupert but they had been for appearances' sake only.

Often Isla felt a complete fraud when she spoke with women about birth control and pelvic floor exercises, or offered advice about love-making during and after pregnancy, when she had never even come close to making love with anyone herself.

Yes, how she would have loved Rupert to be here tonight, to hold her friend's hand and to lean just a little on him as the introductions were made and she stared into the black eyes of a man who actually had the usually very cool Isla feeling just a little bit dizzy.

'Call me Alessi,' he said.

'Sorry, Alessi, I keep forgetting,' Emily said. 'Isla is Head of Midwifery at MMU.'

'It is very nice to meet you,' Alessi said. He held out his hand and Isla offered hers and gave him a smile. His hand was warm as it briefly closed around the ends of her fingers and so, too, were Isla's cheeks. 'Can I get you a drink?' he offered.

'No, thanks.' Isla was about to say that she would get this round but for some reason, even as she shook her head, she changed her mind. 'Actually, yes, please, I'd love a drink. I just promised Cathy, my patient, that I was going to have a glass of champagne for her tonight.'

Alessi headed off to the bar and Emily took the opportunity to have a quick word. 'Isla, thank you for getting here, I know you were held back, but I'm really going to have to get home.'

'Of course,' Isla said. 'I know how hard it is for you to get away and I really appreciate you coming out tonight. The numbers were just so low I didn't want Alessandro, I mean Alessi, to think that nobody could be bothered to greet him. Go home to your babies.'

As Emily said her goodbyes, another colleague nudged Isla. 'Gorgeous, isn't he?'

'I guess.' Isla shrugged her shoulders. She could get away with such a dismissive comment purely because she had Rupert standing in the wings of her carefully stage-managed social life. Isla glanced over to the bar and looked at Alessi, whose back was to her as he ordered her drink. He was wearing black trousers and had a white fitted shirt on that showed off his olive skin. Isla felt a flutter in her stomach as it dawned on her that she was actually checking him out. She took in the toned torso and the long length of his legs but as he turned around she flicked her gaze away and spoke with her colleagues.

'Thank you for that,' Isla said when he handed her her drink. She was a little taken aback when he came and sat on the low sofa beside her, and she took a sip.

Oh!

With all the functions that Isla attended she knew her wines and this was French champagne at its best! 'When I said champagne…' Isla winced because here in Melbourne champagne usually meant sparkling wine. 'You must think me terribly rude.'

'Far from it,' Alessi said. 'It's nice to see someone celebrating.'

Isla nodded. 'I've just been at the most amazing birth,' she admitted, and then, to her complete surprise, she was off—telling Alessi all about Cathy and Dan's long journey and just how wonderful the birth had been. 'I'm sorry,' she said when she realised that they had been talking about it for a good ten minutes. 'I'm going on a bit.'

'I don't blame you,' Alessi said. 'I think there is no greater reward than seeing a family make it against the odds. It is those moments that we treasure and hold onto, to get us through the dark times in our jobs.'

Isla nodded, glad that he seemed to understand just how priceless this evening's birth had been.

They chatted incredibly easily, having to tear themselves away from their conversation to say goodbye to colleagues who were starting to drift off.

'I can't believe that we went to the same

school!' Isla said when Alessi brought it to her attention. 'How old are you?'

'Thirty.'

'So you would have been two years above me…' Isla tried to place him but couldn't—they would, given their age difference, for the most part, have been on separate campuses. 'You might know my older sister Isabel,' Isla said. 'She would have been a couple of years ahead of you.'

'I vaguely remember her. She was head girl when I went to the senior campus. Though I didn't really get involved in the social side—I was there on scholarship so if I wanted to stay there I really had to concentrate on making the grades. Were you head girl, too?'

Isla nodded and laughed, but Alessi didn't.

Alessi was actually having a small private battle with himself as he recalled his private-school days. Alessi and his sister Allegra had been there, as he had just told Isla, on scholarship. Both had endured the taunts of the elite—the glossy, beautiful rich kids who'd felt that he and his sister hadn't belonged at their school. Alessi had for the most part ignored the gibes but when it had got too much for Allegra he would step in. They had both worked in the family café and put up with the smirks from their peers when they'd come in for a coffee on their way to school and found the twins serving. Now Allegra was the one who smirked when her old school friends came into Geo's, an exclusive Greek restaurant in Melbourne, and they realised how well the Manos family had done.

Still, just because they had been on the end of snobby bitchiness it didn't mean that Isla had been like that, Alessi told himself.

They got on really well.

Isla even texted him an image she had on her phone of a school reunion she had gone to a couple of years ago.

'I remember him!' Alessi said, and gave a dry laugh. 'And he would remember me!'

'Meaning?'

'We had a scuffle. He stole my sister's blazer and she was too worried to tell my parents that she'd lost another one.'

'Did you get it back?'

'Oh, yes.' Alessi grinned and then his smile faded as Isla pointed to a woman in the photo who he hadn't seen in a very long time.

'Do you remember Talia?' Isla asked. 'She's a doctor now, though she's moved to Singapore. She actually came all the way back just for the reunion.'

Alessi didn't really comment but, yes, he knew Talia. Her name was still brought up by his parents at times—how wrong he had been to shame her by ending things a couple of days before their engagement. How he could be married now and settled down instead of the casual dates that incensed his family so.

Not a soul, apart from Talia, knew the real reason why they had broken up.

It was strange that there on Isla's phone could

be such a big part of his past and Isla now dragged him back to it.

'She's got four children,' Isla said. 'Four!'

Make that five, Alessi wanted to add, his heart black with recall. He could still vividly remember dropping by to check in on Talia—he'd been concerned that she hadn't been in lectures and that concern had tipped to panic as he'd seen her pale features and her discomfort. Alessi had thought his soon-to-be fiancé might be losing their baby and had insisted that Talia go to hospital. He had just been about to bring the car around when she had told him there was no longer a baby. Since the morning's theatre list at a local clinic he had, without input, no longer been a father-to-be.

Of course, he chose not to say anything to Isla and swiftly moved on, asking about Isla's Debutante Ball, anything other than revisiting the painful past. She showed him another photo and though he still could not place a teenage Isla he asked who an elderly woman in the photo was.

'Our housekeeper, Evie.' Isla gave a fond smile. 'My parents couldn't make it that night but she came. Evie came to all the things that they couldn't get to. She was very sick then, and died a couple of months later. Evie was going to go into a hospice but Isabel and I ended up looking after her at home.'

Isla stared at the image on her phone. She hadn't looked at those photos for a very long time and seeing Evie's loving smile had her remembering a time that she tried not to.

'Would you like another drink?' Alessi offered as Isla put away her phone, both happy to end a difficult trip down memory lane.

'Not for me.'

'Something to eat?'

She was both hungry enough and relaxed with him enough to say yes.

Potato wedges and sour cream had never tasted so good!

In fact, they got on so well that close to midnight both realised it was just the two of them left.

'I'd better go,' Isla said.

'Are you on in the morning?'

'No.' Isla shook her head. 'I'm off for the weekend. I'm pretty much nine to five these days, though I do try to mix it up a bit and do some regular stints on nights.' They walked down the steps and out into the street. 'So you start on Monday?' she checked.

'I do,' Alessi said. 'I'm really looking forward to it. At the last hospital I worked at there was always a struggle for NICU cots and equipment. It is going to be really nice working somewhere that's so cutting-edge.' He looked at Isla—she was seriously stunning and was looking right into his eyes. The attraction between them had been instant and was completely undeniable. Alessi dated, flirted and enjoyed women with absolute ease. 'I'm looking forward to the weekend, too, though.'

'That's right, you're going away with your girlfriend...'

'No,' Alessi said. 'We broke up.'

'I'm sorry,' Isla said, which was the right response.

'I'm not,' Alessi said, which was the wrong response for Isla.

She was terribly aware how unguarded she had been tonight. Perhaps safe in the knowledge that he was seeing someone.

She looked into his black eyes and then her gaze flicked down and she watched as his lips stretched into a slow, lazy smile.

His mouth was seductive and he hadn't yet kissed her but she knew that soon he would.

As his lips first grazed hers Isla's nerves actually started to dissolve like a cube of sugar being dipped into warm coffee—it was sweet, it was pleasurable, it was actually sublime. Such a gentle, skilled kiss, so different from the forced ones with Rupert. It felt like soft butterflies were tickling her lips and Isla realised that her mouth was moving naturally with his.

Alessi's hands were on her hips, she could feel his warm hands through her denim shorts and she wanted more pressure, wanted more of something that she didn't know how to define, she simply didn't want it to end. But as the kiss naturally deepened, her eyes snapped open and she pulled back. Her first taste of tongue was shocking enough, but that she was kissing a man in the street was for Isla more terrifying.

He thought her easy, Isla was sure, panic building within her about where this might lead. She almost *was* easy with him because for the first time in her life she now knew how a kiss could lead straight to bed.

She had many weapons of self-defence in her armoury but she leapt straight for the big one and shot Alessi a look of absolute distaste.

'What the hell do you think you're doing?' she snapped, even if she had been a very willing participant. 'I was just trying to be friendly…'

Alessi quickly realised that he *had* been right to be cautious about her.

He knew the looks she was giving him well.

Very well!

She didn't actually say the words—*do you know who I am?* Though Isla's expression most certainly did. It was a snobby, derisive look, it was a get-your-hands-off-me-you-poor-Greek-boy look.

'My mistake,' Alessi shrugged. 'Goodnight, Isla.'

He promptly walked off—he wasn't going to hang around to be trampled on.

Her loss.

Alessi knew she'd enjoyed the kiss as much as he had and that her mouth, her body had invited more. He simply knew.

Isla *had* enjoyed their kiss.

As she climbed into a taxi she was scalding with embarrassment but there was another feeling, too—despite the appalling ending to tonight her lips were still warm from Alessi's and her body felt a little bit alive for the very first time, a touch awoken to what had seemed impossible before.

As she let herself into her flat, a gorgeous penthouse with a view of Melbourne that rivalled that of the Rooftop Bar, she smiled at Isabel.

'Sorry I didn't get there,' Isabel said. 'Did you have a good night?'

Isla, still flushed from his kiss, still a little shaken inside, nodded.

It had, in fact, been the best Valentine's night of her life.

Not that Alessi could ever know.

CHAPTER ONE

NEW YEAR'S DAY.

Isla saw the sign for the turn-off to Melbourne International Airport and carried on with her conversation as if she and Isabel were popping out for breakfast.

They were both trying to ignore the fact that Isabel was heading to live in England for a year and so, instead of talking about that, they chatted about Rupert. He was back in Melbourne for a week and the *supposed* news had broken that he'd had a fling with one of the actresses in his latest film. Not even Isabel knew that Isla's relationship with Rupert was a ruse.

'You're truly not upset?' Isabel checked, and Isla, who wore her mask well, just laughed as she turned off the freeway.

'What, I'm supposed to be upset because reports say that he got off with some actress in America a few weeks ago?' Isla shook her head. 'It doesn't bother me. I couldn't care less what they say in some magazine.'

'You're so much tougher than I am,' Isabel sighed. 'I simply can't imagine how I would feel if…' Her voice trailed off.

The conversation they had perhaps been trying to avoid was getting closer and closer and neither wanted to face it.

Isla knew what Isabel had been about to say.

She couldn't stand to hear about Sean if he was with someone else.

Sean Anderson, an obstetrician, had been working at the Victoria since November and was the reason they were at the airport now. Sean was the reason that Isabel had accepted a professional exchange with Darcie Green and was heading for Cambridge, just to escape the re-emergence of her childhood sweetheart into her life.

The large multistorey car park at the airport had never made Isla feel sick before but it did today.

They unloaded Isabel's cases from the boot, found a trolley and then headed to the elevator. Once inside Isla pressed the button for the departure floor and forced a smile at her sister as they stood in the lift.

'If Darcie's flight gets in on time you might have time to see her,' Isla said, and Isabel nodded.

'She sounds really nice from her emails. Well, I hope she is, for your sake, given that she's going to be sharing the flat with you.'

Isla had never lived alone and so, with her older sister heading overseas and as their flat was so huge, it had seemed the perfect idea at the time. Now, though, Isla wasn't so sure. Isabel was going away to sort her heart out and Isla was going to do the same. She really wanted things to be different this year, she wanted to finally start getting on with her life, and that meant dating.

That meant letting her guard down and dropping Rupert and, despite being terrified, Isla was also determined to bring on a necessary change.

Not tonight, though!

Tonight there were drinks to greet Darcie at the Rooftop Bar and Alessi would be there.

It was almost a year since that Valentine's night and since then the atmosphere between them had been strained at best. He was a playboy and made no excuse about it and Isla loathed his flirting and casual dating of her staff, though he barely glanced in her direction, let alone flirted with her. Alessi, it was clear, considered Isla to be a stuck-up cow who had somehow wormed her way into her senior position thanks to her father. They rarely worked together and that suited them both.

The early morning sun was very low and bright as Isla and Isabel crossed the tunnel that would take them from the car park to the departure lounge. A few heads turned as the sisters walked by. It wasn't just that they were both blonde and good-looking but that, thanks to their frequent appearances in the celebrity pages of newspapers and magazines, people recognised them.

Isabel and Isla were more than used to it but it felt especially invasive this morning.

Today they weren't minor celebrities but were sisters who were saying goodbye for a whole year, for a reason even *they* could not discuss—an event that had happened twelve years ago. Something that both women had fought to put behind them, though, for both, it had proved impossible.

What had happened that night had scarred them both in different ways, Isla thought as she watched Isabel check her baggage in.

She didn't really know Isabel's scars, she just knew that they were there.

They had to be.

Isla forced a smile as Isabel came back from the check-in desk.

'I'm not going to wait to meet Darcie,' Isabel said, and Isla nodded. Yes, they could stand around and talk, or perhaps go and get a coffee and extend the goodbye, but it was all just too painful. 'I think I'll just go through customs now.'

'Look out, England!' Isla attempted a little joke but then her voice cracked as they both realised that this was it. 'I'm going to miss you so much!' Isla said. She would. They not only worked and lived together but shared in the exhausting round of charity events and social engagements that took place when you were a Delamere girl.

They shared everything except a rehash of that awful night but here, on this early summer morning, for the first time it was tentatively broached. 'You understand I have to go, don't you?' Isabel asked.

Isla nodded, not trusting herself to speak.

'I don't know how to be around him,' Isabel admitted. 'Now that Sean is back, I just don't know how to deal with it. I know that he doesn't understand why I ended our relationship so abruptly.

We both knew it was more than a teenage crush, he was the love of my life…' Tears were pouring down Isabel's cheeks and even though she was younger than Isabel, again, it was Isla who knew she had to be strong. She pushed aside her own hurts and fears and cuddled her big sister and told her that she was making the right choice, that she would be okay and that she could get through this.

'I know how hard it's been for you since he came to MMU,' Isla said.

'You won't say anything to Sean…'

'Oh, please,' Isla said. 'I'd never tell anyone, ever. I promised you that a long time ago. You've got this year to sort yourself out and I'm going to do the same.'

'You?' Isabel said in surprise. 'What could you possibly have to sort out? I've never known anyone more together than you.'

Isla, though, knew that she wasn't together. 'I love you,' she said, instead of answering the question.

'I love you, too.'

They had another hug and then Isla stood and watched as her sister headed towards customs and showed her passport and boarding pass. Just as she went past the point of no return Isabel paused and turned briefly and waved at a smiling Isla.

Only when Isabel had gone did Isla's smile disappear and Isla, who never cried, felt the dam breaking then. She was so grateful that she had an hour before Darcie arrived because she would need every minute of it to compose herself. As she walked back through the tunnel towards the car Isla could hardly see where she was going because her eyes were swimming in tears, but somehow she made it back to the car and climbed in and sat there and cried like she never had in her life.

Yes, she fully understood why Isabel had to get away now that Sean had returned. The memories of that time were so painful that they could still awake Isla in the middle of the night. She fully understood, with Sean reappearing, how hard it must be for Isabel to see him every day on the maternity unit.

It was agony for Isla, too.

She sat there in her car, remembering the excitement of being twelve years old and listening to a sixteen-year-old Isabel telling her about her boyfriend and dating and kissing. Isla had listened intently, hanging onto every word, but then Isabel had suddenly stopped telling her things.

A plane roared overhead and the sob that came from Isla was so deep and so primal it was as if she were back there—waking to the sound of her sister's tears and the aftermath, except this time she was able to cry about it.

Their parents had been away for a weekend. Evie, their housekeeper, had lived in a small apartment attached to the house and so, effectively, they had been alone. Isla, on waking to the sounds of her sister crying, had got out of bed and padded to the bathroom and stood outside, listening for a moment.

'Isabel?' Isla knocked on the bathroom door.

'Go away, Isla,' Isabel said, then let out very low groan and Isla realised that her sister was in pain.

'Isabel,' Isla called. 'Unlock the door and let me in.'

Silence.

But then came another low moan that had Isla gripped with fear.

'Isabel, please.' She knocked on the door again, only this time with urgency. 'If you don't let me in then I'm going to go and get Evie.'

Evie was so much more than a housekeeper. She looked after the two girls as if they were her own. She worried about them, was there for them while their parents attended their endless parties.

They both loved her.

Isla was just about to run and get Evie when the door was unlocked and Isla let herself in. She stepped inside the bathroom and couldn't believe what she saw. Isabel was drenched in sweat and there was blood on the tiles, but as she watched her sister fold over it dawned on Isla what was happening.

Isabel was giving birth.

'Please don't tell Evie,' Isabel begged. 'No one must know, Isla, you have to promise me that you will never tell anyone…'

Somehow, despite the blood, despite the terror and the moans from her sister, Isla stayed calm.

She knew what she had to do.

Isla dropped down to her knees on instinct rather than fear as Isabel lay back on the floor, lifting herself up on her elbows. 'It's okay, Isabel,' Isla said reassuringly. 'It's going to be okay.'

'There's something between my legs…' Isabel groaned. 'It's coming.'

Isla had been born a midwife, she knew that then. It was strange but even at that tender age, somehow Isla dealt with the unfolding events. She looked down at the tiny scrap that had been born to her hands and managed to stay calm as an exhausted Isabel wept.

He was dead, that much Isla knew, yet he was perfect. His little eyes were fused closed and he was so very still.

Tomorrow she would start to doubt herself. Tomorrow she would wonder if there was something more that she could have done for him. In the months and years ahead Isla would terrorise herself with those very questions and would go over and over holding her little nephew in her hands instead of doing more. But there, in that moment, in the still of the bathroom, Isla knew.

She wrapped her tiny nephew in a small hand towel. There was the placenta and the cord still attached and she continued to hold him as Isabel lay on the floor, sobbing.

'He's beautiful,' Isla said. He was. She gazed upon his features as her fingers held his tiny, tiny hands and she looked at his spindly arms and cuddled him and then, when Isabel was ready, Isla handed the tiny baby to her.

'Did you know you were pregnant?' Isla asked,

but Isabel said nothing, just stared at her tiny baby and stroked his little cheek.

'Does Sean know?' Isla asked.

'No one knows,' Isabel said. 'No one is ever to know about this.' She looked at Isla, her eyes urgent. 'You have to promise me that you will never, ever tell anyone.'

Some promises were too big to make, though.

'I have to tell Evie,' Isla said.

'Isla, please, no one must know.'

'And so what are we supposed to do with him?' Isla demanded.

'I don't know.'

'You know what you *don't* want me to do, though. You know that he needs to be properly taken care of,' Isla said, and Isabel nodded tearfully.

'You won't tell anyone else,' Isabel sobbed. 'Promise me, Isla.'

'I promise.'

Isla sped through the house and to Evie. The elderly housekeeper was terribly distressed at first, but then she calmed down and dealt with things. She understood, better than most, the scandal this might cause and the terrible impact it would have on Isabel if it ever got out. She had a sister who worked in a hospital in the outer suburbs and Evie called her and asked what to do.

Isla sat, her tears still flowing as she recalled the drive out of the city to the suburbs. Isabel was holding the tiny baby and crying beside her till the lights of the hospital came into view. Evie's sister met them and Isabel was put in a wheelchair and taken to Maternity, with Isla following behind. The midwife who had greeted them had been so lovely to Isabel, just so calm, wise and efficient.

'What happens now?' Isla asked. It was as if only then had they noticed that Isabel's young sister was there and she was shown to a small waiting room.

It had been the last time Isla had seen her nephew.

She didn't really know what had gone on.

Evie had come in at one point and said that the baby was too small to be registered. Isla hadn't known what that meant other than that no one would have to find out.

Her parents would later question Isla's decision to become a midwife. They had deemed that it wasn't good enough for a Delamere girl but Isla had stood by her calling.

She'd wanted to be as kind and as calm as the staff had been with Isabel that night.

With one modification.

Though her sister had been gently dealt with by midwives who had been used to terrified sixteen-year-old girls who did not want their parents to find out, one person had been forgotten.

Isla had sat alone and unnoticed in the waiting room.

Now she knew things should have been handled differently—the midwives, the obstetrician, at least one of them should have recognised Isla's terror and spoken at length with her about what had happened. They should have come in and taken care of the twelve-year-old girl who had just delivered her dead nephew. They should have carefully explained that the baby had been born at around eighteen weeks gestation, which had meant that there was nothing Isla could have possibly done to save him.

It would be many years before Isla got those answers and she'd had to find them out for herself.

Yes, that night had left scars.

Despite appearances, despite her immaculate clothes and long glossy hair and seemingly spectacular social life, Isla had equated sex with disaster. Not logically, of course, but throughout her teenage years she had avoided dating boys and in her final year at school Rupert had seemed the perfect solution. Still she'd kept the secret of that night to herself.

She had promised her sister after all.

CHAPTER TWO

ISLA DID WHAT she could to repair the damage to her face—her eyelids were puffy, her nose was red and her lips swollen. Isla never cried. Even at the most difficult births she was very aware that even a single tear might lead back to that memory and so she kept her emotions in check.

Always.

She put on some sunglasses and made her way to Arrivals, where she stood, her eyes moving between the three exit doors and wondering if she would even recognise Darcie when she came out.

As it turned out, it was Darcie who recognised her.

'Isla!' Her name was called from behind the

rail and the second she turned Isla's face broke into a smile.

'I was watching the wrong door.' Isla greeted Darcie with a hug. 'Happy New Year,' she said.

'Happy New Year, to you, too.' Darcie smiled.

'I was starting to worry that I wouldn't recognise you when you came out,' Isla admitted.

'Well, I certainly recognised you. You're as gorgeous as you are in the magazine I was just…' Darcie's voice trailed off and she went a bit pink, perhaps guessing that the article she had read on the plane might not be Isla's favourite topic, given that it had revealed Rupert's infidelity.

Isla let that comment go and they stepped out into the morning sun. Melbourne was famous for its fickle weather but this morning the sky was silver blue and the sun had been firmly turned on to welcome Darcie.

'It shouldn't take too long to get home,' Isla said as they hit the morning rush-hour traffic. 'Did you get much sleep on the plane?'

'Not really.' Darcie shook her head. 'I shan't be much company today.'

'That's fine.' Isla smiled. 'I'm dropping you home and then I'll be going into work so you'll have the place to yourself.'

'You should have told me that you were working this morning!' Darcie said. 'I could have taken a taxi. You didn't have to come out to the airport to meet me.'

'It was no problem and I was there anyway to see Isabel off.'

'Oh, of course you were.' Darcie glanced at Isla. Despite the repair job that Isla had done with make-up and dark glasses, it was quite clear to Darcie that she had been crying. Now, though, Darcie thought she knew why. 'It must have been hard to say goodbye to your sister.'

'It was,' Isla admitted. 'I'm going to miss her a lot, though I bet she's going to have an amazing year in England.'

They chatted easily as they drove into Melbourne. Isla pointed out a few landmarks—Federation Square and the Arts Centre—and Darcie said she couldn't wait to get on a tram.

'We'll be catching one tonight,' Isla told her. 'I've organised for some colleagues to get together and have drinks tonight. It's a bit of a tradition on the maternity unit that we all try to get together before a new staff member starts, just so we can get most of the introductions out of the way and everything. If it's too much for you, given how far you've flown, everyone will understand.'

'No, it won't be too much, that sounds lovely. I'm looking forward to meeting everyone.'

'Have you left a boyfriend behind?' Isla asked, and Darcie shook her head.

'No, I'm recently single and staying that way. I'm here to focus on my career. I've heard so much about the MMU at the Victoria—I just can't wait to get started.'

'There it is.' Isla drove slowly past the hospital where Darcie would commence work the next day. It was a gorgeous old building that, contrary to outer appearances, was equipped with the best staff and equipment that modern medicine had to offer.

They soon pulled into the underground car park of the apartment block and took the lift to the penthouse.

'Wow,' Darcie said as they stepped inside. 'When you said that we'd be sharing a flat…' She was clearly a bit taken aback by the rather luxurious surroundings and looked out of the floor-to-ceiling windows to the busy city below. 'It's stunning.'

'It will soon feel like home,' Isla assured her. 'I'll give you a quick tour but then I really need to get to work.'

'There's no need for a tour,' Darcie said. 'I'll just be having a very quick shower and then bed. I'll probably still be in it when you get home.'

Isla showed Darcie to her room. It had its own en suite and Isla briefly went through how to use the remote control for the blinds and a few other things and then she quickly got changed to head into work. 'I'll try and get back about six o'clock,' Isla said. 'I've told people to get there about seven, but if I do get stuck at work I'll send a colleague to pick you up.'

'There's no need for that.' Darcie was clearly very independent, Isla realised. 'Just tell me the name of the bar and if you can't make it home in time, I'll find my own way there.'

Isla smiled, though she shook her head. 'I'm not leaving you to make your own way there on your first day in Melbourne.'

Darcie was nice, Isla decided as she drove to work. She still felt a little bit unsettled from her breakdown earlier. She had never cried like that. In fact, she did everything she could not to think about that terrible morning. The trouble was, though, since Sean had arrived, that long-ago time seemed to be catching up with both Isabel and her. As if to prove her point, the first person she saw when she walked into MMU was Sean. With no dark glasses to hide behind now, Isla's heart sank a little when he called her over.

'I was wondering if you could have a word with Christine Adams for me,' Sean said. 'I know how good you are with teenagers and, in all honesty, nothing I say about contraception seems to be getting through to her. At this rate, Christine is going to be back here in nine months' time. I inserted an IUD after delivery but, as you know, she had a small haemorrhage and it's been expelled so I can't put another one in for six weeks. She's also got a history of deep vein thrombosis so she's not able to go on the Pill. Can you just reiterate to her and her boyfriend that they need to use condoms every time? She's told me that she doesn't want another baby for a couple of years, and I think she's right—her body needs a rest.'

'She's very anaemic, isn't she?' Isla checked.

'She is. I was considering a transfusion when she bled but she's going to try and get her iron up herself.'

'I'll have a chat,' Isla agreed. She was very used to dealing with young mums and last year had started a group called Teenage Mums-To-Be, or TMTB, as it was known. Even though she couldn't always be there to take the group, one of the other midwives would run it for her if necessary and they often had an obstetrician come along to talk to the young women, too. It was proving to be a huge success.

Christine had attended TMTB for two babies in one year. Robbie, who had been born a couple of days ago, was her second baby. This morning Christine was going home to look after a new-born *and* a ten-month-old with her iron level in her boots. Isla knew that Sean was right, she could be back again at the MMU very soon.

'One other thing, Isla,' Sean started as Isla went to head off, but whatever he'd been about to say was put on hold as he looked over Isla's shoulder. 'Good morning, Alessi, thanks for coming down—you're looking very smart.'

Especially smart, Isla thought! Alessi's good looks and easy smile she did not need this morning, especially as he was looking particularly divine. He was dressed in an extremely impressive suit, his tie was immaculately knotted and he was, for once, freshly shaven. He might as well be on his way to a wedding rather than dropping into the unit to check a newborn that Sean was worried about.

'Good morning, all,' Alessi said.

'Morning, Alessi,' one of Isla's midwives called.

'Looking good,' someone else commented, and Isla bristled as she heard a wolf whistle come from the treatment room.

They were like bees to honey around him and Alessi took it all in his stride and just smiled, though it did not fall in Isla's direction. They didn't get on. Of course they were professional when they worked together. Their paths often crossed but they both tried to make sure that there was as little contact as possible. His flirting with her staff annoyed the hell out of Isla, however, and she was very tempted to have a word with him about it. She had recently found out that he was dating one of her students, Amber.

That made it sound worse than it was, Isla knew—Amber was a mature-age student and older than she herself was, but even so, Isla wasn't impressed.

What she couldn't dispute, though, was that Alessi was one of the hardest-working doctors she had ever known. As hard as he dated, he worked. He was there in the mornings when she arrived and often long after she went home.

'What do you have for me?' Alessi asked Sean, but before he could answer Isla made to go.

'I'll leave you both to it,' Isla said.

'Could you hold on a second, Isla? I still want to speak with you,' Sean said, thwarting her attempt to make a swift getaway. He turned to Alessi. 'I've got a baby I delivered in the early hours. He seemed to be fine when delivered but there's no audible cry now. All observations are normal and he seems well other than he isn't making much noise when he cries.'

'I'll take a look.' Alessi nodded.

'So why are you all dressed up?' Sean asked,

given that Alessi usually dressed in scrubs and looked as if he had just rolled out of bed.

'I'm having lunch today with the bigwigs...' Alessi rolled his eyes and then they did meet Isla's and he gave her a tight smile. 'I'm actually having lunch with Isla's father.'

She couldn't quite put her finger on it but Isla knew that he was having a little dig at her.

'Enjoy,' Isla said.

'I shan't,' Alessi tartly replied. 'Sometimes you have to just suffer through these things.'

The lunch that Alessi was speaking about was due to the fact that he was soon to be receiving an award in recognition of his contributions to the neonatal unit over the past year. There was a huge fundraising ball being held in a couple of weeks' time and Charles Delamere was attempting to push Alessi towards the charitable side of things—hence the lunch today, where it would be strongly suggested that Alessi, with his good looks and easy smile, might be a more visible presence. While Alessi knew how essential fundraising was and felt proud to have his achievements acknowledged, a part of him resented having to walk the talk. He'd far rather be getting on with the job than appearing on breakfast television to speak about the neonatal unit, as Charles had recently suggested.

Alessi chatted for a moment more with Sean but, during that brief exchange with Isla, he had noted the puffiness around her eyes and had guessed, rightly, that she had been crying. He was wrong about the reason, though. Alessi assumed Isla's tears were because of the weekend reports about her boyfriend's philandering. Even if she was upset there was still plenty of the ice-cold Isla, Alessi thought as she stood there. Her stance was bored and dismissive and she didn't even deign to give him a glance as he headed off to examine the infant.

Isla was anything but bored, though. Seemingly together, she was shaking inside as Alessi walked off because she knew that Sean was going to ask her about Isabel.

'How was this morning?' Sean asked.

'Fine.'

'Isabel got off okay?'

'She just texted to say that she's boarding.' Isla nodded and then did her best to change the subject. 'What did you want to speak with me about?'

'Just that,' Sean answered. 'Isla, my working here didn't have any part in her decision—'

'Sean, Isabel was offered a year's secondment in England. Who wouldn't give their right arm for that?'

'It just—'

'I'm too busy to stand here, chatting,' Isla said, and walked off.

Yes, she could be aloof at times but it was surely better to be thought of as that than to stand discussing Isabel's leaving with Sean.

Isla went to the store cupboard and got some samples of condoms. She put them in a bag and then headed in to speak with Christine, who was there with Blake, her boyfriend, who was also eighteen. Little Joel, their older baby, was also there.

Isla was usually incredibly comfortable approaching such subjects with her patients. She discussed contraception many times a day both on the ward and in the postnatal clinic but when she walked behind the curtains, where Christine was nursing her baby, she also saw Alessi's shoes gleaming beneath the other side of the curtains. That he was examining the baby in the next bed to Christine made Isla feel just a little bit self-conscious.

'Hi, there, Christine.' Isla smiled. 'Hi, Blake. I hear that you're all going home this morning?'

'I can't wait to get him home,' Christine said, and gazed down at Robbie. He was latched onto Christine's breast, beautifully and happily feeding away.

'You're doing so well,' Isla commented. 'You're still feeding Joel, aren't you?'

'Just at night,' Christine replied, 'though he's jealous and wants me all the time now, too.'

Isla glanced over at Joel, who was staring at his new brother with a very put-out look on his face. Christine really was an amazing mum, but Isla could well understand Sean's concern and why he was asking her to reiterate what he had said. Christine was incredibly pale and breast-feeding a newborn and a ten-month-old would certainly take its toll. 'I wanted to have a word with you about contraception—'

'Oh, we've already been spoken to about that,' Christine interrupted. 'The midwife said something this morning and Dr Sean has been in, so you really don't need to explain things again.'

'I do.'

'I'll leave you to it, then.' Blake went to stand but Isla shook her head.

'Oh, no.' Isla smiled as Blake reluctantly sat down. 'I want to speak with both of you. As you know, the IUD insertion didn't work. That happens sometimes, but now it's better that the doctor waits for your six-week checkup to put another in.'

'Dr Sean has explained that,' Christine sighed.

'You do know that you can't rely on breast-feeding as a form of contraception,' Isla gently reminded them, and Christine started to laugh as she looked down at Robbie.

'I know that now—given that I'm holding the proof.'

'And you understand that you can't take the Pill because of your history of blood clots,' Isla continued as Christine vaguely smiled and nodded. She really wasn't taking any of this in. 'You need to use condoms every time, or not have intercourse...'

'There's always the morning-after pill,' Christine said, and Isla shook her head. Privately she didn't like the morning-after pill, unless it was after an episode of abuse, not that she would ever push her own beliefs onto her patients. It was the fact that Christine had a history of blood clots that ruled it out for her and Isla told her so. 'You need to be careful—' Isla started, but Christine interrupted again.

'I'm not waiting six weeks and he…' she nodded her head in Blake's direction '…certainly can't wait that long.'

'I'm not asking you both to wait till then,' Isla said patiently. 'Though you don't *have* to have penetrative sex, there are other things you can do.' Christine just rolled her eyes and Isla ploughed on. 'If you are going to have sex before the IUD is put in then you are to use condoms each and every time.' She looked at Blake. 'That's why I asked to speak to you, too.'

'Oh, leave him alone.' Christine grinned.

'Christine, you're very anaemic and the last thing your body needs now is another pregnancy. I'm just asking Blake to make sure that he's careful.'

'It's not his fault, he tries to be careful,' Christine said, happy to leap to Blake's defence. 'Haven't you ever got so carried away that you just don't care, Isla?'

Isla glanced at the shoes on the other side of the curtain and just knew that Alessi could hear every word and was no doubt having a little laugh.

Rarely, her cheeks were pink as she looked back at Christine.

'Well?' Christine demanded. 'I think you know what I'm talking about, Isla.'

'But this isn't about me,' Isla answered calmly. 'I've raided the store cupboard.' She handed Blake what would hopefully be adequate supplies. 'One each time!' Isla said. 'Or I'll be seeing see you very soon. Perhaps with twins this time, wouldn't that be nice? Four under two, what fun!'

She saw Blake blink and he glanced at Christine and then back at Isla, and hopefully the message had sunk in. 'Got it?' Isla said.

'Got it,' Blake agreed.

As she left them to go through their goody bag she walked straight into Alessi, who was wearing a smile, and there was an extremely rare truce because all Isla could do was let out a little laugh.

'You didn't answer the question, Isla,' Alessi teased.

'No, I didn't.'

'A case of do as I say, not as I do?' Alessi nudged and Isla gave a non-committal smile. He'd die on the spot if he knew the truth but thankfully the small armistice was soon over and Alessi got back to talking about work, which Isla knew better how to handle. 'I'm very happy with the baby that Sean just asked me to see. There's no sign of infection—I think he has a floppy larynx, which is causing the husky cry. Still, I'm going to do a blood test and can his temperature be checked every two hours? Any deterioration at all then I'm to be called straight away.' He watched as Isla nodded and he again took in her puffy eyes and was tempted to say something.

But what could he say?

I'm sorry to hear that your boyfriend's been screwing around on you again?

Alessi wasn't sorry.

Well, perhaps he was sorry for the hurt that had been dished out to Isla but he wasn't sorry that her relationship with Rupert was over.

Close to a year on, despite not particularly *liking* her, Alessi still found himself thinking about that night.

Still, despite her cool disdain, despite having been born with a silver spoon in her mouth, as opposed to the plastic café one that he had been born to, he could not quite get her out of his head.

'What time is everybody meeting tonight?' he asked.

'About seven.'

'Good. Shall I see you there?'

'You shall.'

This was as close to a personal conversation they'd had since that night.

And that was how it would remain, he decided as he walked off.

He didn't like his attraction to her, didn't like that eleven months on, the scent of her was a familiar one whenever they were close, and he didn't like that, despite trying not to, today he had found himself with no choice but to smile into her eyes.

Stay back, Alessi, he told himself.

He liked to keep things light with women. Since Talia he hadn't liked to get too involved. But all that aside, Alessi was determined that Isla Delamere would not be changing her mind on him twice.

CHAPTER THREE

ISLA GOT CAUGHT up in a delivery and didn't make it home until well after six, but Darcie was up and it was actually nice not to come back to an empty flat but share in a glass of wine as they got ready.

'Can I borrow your hair dryer?' Darcie asked. 'The adapter that I brought isn't working.'

'Sure,' Isla said, and went and got it. 'I'll just text Rupert and let him know that I'm running a bit late and to meet us there.'

'Oh, so you're still seeing each—' Darcie abruptly halted whatever it was she'd been about to say. 'I'm so sorry, Isla. That is absolutely none of my business. I think I must have left my manners in England!'

'It's fine.' Isla shrugged. 'My sister said pretty

much the same thing this morning. Look, it really isn't awkward. I don't get upset by what's said in the magazines, they're full of rubbish and lies…'

'Of course they are. It's nice that you can trust him.' Darcie smiled but Isla could see a small flicker of pity in her eyes and knew that Darcie, like everybody else, assumed that Isla was being taken for a fool.

Isla went to have a very quick shower, though perhaps it wasn't quite as quick as the one she had intended to have.

New Year, new start, Isla decided as she soaped up.

She *was* going to break up with Rupert.

Isla already knew that she had to stop hiding behind him and certainly she didn't like it that people thought she was somehow standing by her man as Rupert seemingly made a fool of her.

Rupert had rung and explained what had happened before the news had hit. The actress had the same agent as Rupert and the supposed tell-all had been at the agent's direction. Only when the exposé had happened had Rupert found out it had been planned.

'Not good enough,' Isla had said. Still, she found it hard to be cross with him—after all, she knew that what had been said in the article was all lies.

Isla was determined to end it, though she was tempted to put off the break-up. She had asked Rupert to stick close to her tonight and she was nervous about the charity ball coming up in a couple of weeks. Alessi's award meant that he would be sitting at the same table as her father—the same table as her!

Yet things had seemed better when they'd spoken today, Isla thought, recalling the smile he had given as she'd come out from behind Christine's curtain. She closed her eyes for a moment and remembered their kiss that night and just how nice it had been to briefly be in his arms. She stood in the shower, the water cascading over her, as she returned to the blissful memory.

Her hands moved over her hips as she remembered his there, and then her eyes snapped open as one hand started to move down of its own accord as she ached, honestly ached to return to the memory and bring it to a more fitting conclusion. She wanted to know what might have happened had she not said no. She wanted to explore the possibilities, her body was almost begging her to.

Isla stood, stunned by her own arousal.

She had buried her sexuality completely.

Since the night she'd delivered Isabel's baby she'd just quashed that side of herself.

Now, though, her breasts felt so heavy she was fighting herself not to touch them and the intense ache between her legs refused to recede. For the first time she wanted to explore her own body.

Shocked, Isla turned off the shower taps and stepped out. She quickly dried herself and pulled on some underwear and dressed. She wore a very pale green summer dress that did nothing to reduce the flush on her cheeks. She simply couldn't stop thinking about Alessi and that he'd be there tonight and so, too, that smile.

And the memory of that kiss.

He'd use you, Isla reminded herself as she put on lip gloss. The same way he'd worked his way through half of MMU.

Not that any of the staff seemed to regret their flings with Alessi.

Would she regret one?

Isla snapped herself out of it.

There was no way she was going to do anything about the reluctant torch she carried for Alessi. She could actually picture his incredulous smile if she told him her truth. Scrap that, incredulous laughter, she amended, and then headed out to the lounge.

'You look great.' Darcie smiled. 'I'm actually nervous about meeting everyone.'

'Well, don't be,' Isla said. 'They're a friendly bunch.'

It was a warm, sultry night and they took a

tram for a couple of stops and then arrived at the bar and, as promised, everybody was incredibly friendly and pleased to meet the new obstetrician.

'This is Lucas,' Isla introduced them. 'He's a senior midwife on the MMU...'

'It's nice to meet you,' Darcie said with a smile, and Isla continued the introductions.

'And this is Sophia, a community midwife...' Thankfully, for Isla, Alessi wasn't there, and she allowed herself to relax. She went and bought some drinks and ordered a couple of bottles for the table but as she walked back she saw Alessi had just arrived. What gnawed at Isla was that he was there with Amber.

'This is Alessi.' Isla pushed out a smile. 'He's a neonatologist. Alessi, this is Darcie...' She watched as he smiled his killer smile at Darcie and then Isla continued. 'And this Amber, a *student* midwife...' Isla almost winced as she heard the tart note to her voice and she caught Alessi's eye. She wasn't jealous that he was dating her student; she wanted to tell him instead that she was cross.

'Hi, there.' Isla jumped as she heard Rupert's voice and felt his arm come around her waist. 'Sorry if I'm a bit late.'

'It's fine.' Isla had never been more pleased to see him and gave him a kiss—the practised kiss that they were both used to. What she wasn't so used to was turning back to the table and the black look Alessi was throwing in Rupert's direction.

He looked then at Isla and gave the smallest shake of his head.

All evening she found herself aware of his disapproval.

Well, she very much disapproved of who Alessi was dating, too.

Her skin prickled when he spoke with Amber. Her usually cool edge seemed to be melting and though the conversation flowed at the table, for once Isla wasn't the perfect hostess. Thankfully everybody was keen to hear about how things worked in Cambridge, where Darcie was from and where Isabel would now be working. No one, apart from Rupert and Alessi, seemed to notice her tension.

'Take it easy,' Rupert said, because Isla was again topping up her glass. Isla rarely drank more than one glass of champagne but tonight she was rather grateful for the wine, and Rupert, who could sense her volatility, was right to warn her.

Not that Alessi approved of Rupert telling her what to do—Isla saw the sharp rise of his eyebrows at Rupert's words.

Alessi didn't like it that Rupert, given what he was putting her through, had just warned Isla to slow down. He didn't like it that Rupert was here in the least. Alessi was, in fact, having an extremely uncomfortable evening, though it wasn't Isla that he felt bad for, but Amber. Alessi, even if his relationships didn't last very long, would never cheat or flirt with another woman, except his mind was fighting not to do just that.

It felt wrong to be sitting with Amber while Isla was there.

He was very aware that he was sitting next to the wrong woman.

'I'm just going to go to the loo,' Isla said, and as she got up to leave, Alessi made himself sit there, though the temptation was to follow her.

The restrooms were located right on the other side of the bar and Isla headed off. She knew she had maybe had a little bit too much to drink and was glad of the chance to just take a breath.

No one had said a word about Rupert. They were all used to Isla bringing him along but she was aware of slight pity in her colleagues' eyes and Isla loathed it.

Tonight she *was* ending it, which left her without a safety net, and as she walked out of the loos and straight into Alessi the Rupert-free tightrope got its first wobble, the first inkling of what was to come.

'Everything okay?' Alessi asked, because the look that she gave him was less than pleasant.

'Actually, no,' Isla said. 'What are you doing, dating one of my students?'

'Excuse me?'

'You heard.'

'She isn't *my* student,' Alessi pointed out. 'You're talking as if Amber's eighteen when, in fact, she's a thirty-two-year-old single mother of two. I'm hardly leading her astray—'

'I don't like the way you flirt with my midwives,' Isla interrupted, and Alessi gave her a slow smile, though his eyes told her he was less than impressed with what she was saying.

'Have there been any complaints?'

'Of course not.'

'Any hint as to inappropriateness on my part?' Alessi checked, and watched Isla's cheeks turn to fire as she shook her head. 'Then I'd tread very carefully here if I were you, Isla,' he said. 'The staff don't have an issue?' He raised an eyebrow and Isla gave a terse shake of her head. 'And I don't have an issue,' he drawled. 'So, in fact, the only person who has a problem with my dating Amber is you. I wonder why that is?'

Isla stood, her face flaming. She knew that she shouldn't have said anything, especially not tonight, but now that she had it was impossible to take it back. 'I'm just letting you know how I feel about the issue.'

'What issue?'

Isla licked her tense lips as he backed her to the wall but her lack of response didn't end the conversation.

'I flirt, Isla. I date. I enjoy women but only women who get that it's only ever going to be short-term…'

'Why?'

The question was out before she considered it but it was pertinent enough to halt Alessi in his tracks.

Why?

It was a question few, outside the family, asked him. A question he had never truthfully answered and he had no intention of doing so now.

'Because that is how I choose to live my life. I don't need your approval, or you to rubber-stamp who I date from MMU, but I can tell you now I have never once cheated on anyone. I don't have to make up lies or excuses about what's been said or where I've been…'

'I need to get back,' Isla said, not liking where this conversation was leading, but Alessi wouldn't let her off the hook.

'We've only just started talking,' he said. 'And given you're so inclined to discuss my sex life, I'm sure you won't mind if I share my feelings about yours. Have some respect for yourself…' He met her eyes and Isla took a sharp breath as he now voiced what nobody else had had the guts to. 'What are you with him for, Isla? It's all over the internet and plastered across every magazine that he's screwing around and yet you're carrying on as if nothing's happened.'

'It's none of your business.'

'Well, I'm making it mine,' Alessi said. 'Why would you let him treat you like that?' He looked over as Rupert came around the corner and stood for a moment as he witnessed the angry confrontation.

'There you are,' Rupert said, and, having been instructed by Isla to stay close, he came and put an arm around her waist, dropping a kiss on her head. 'Darcie is starting to droop. I think she might need to go home.'

'Sure,' Isla said as Alessi just stood there, staring at Rupert with a challenge in his eyes. 'If you can tell Darcie that I'll be there in a few minutes, that would be great. I just need to discuss something with Alessi.'

As Rupert walked off Alessi's angry eyes met Isla's. 'He's got a nerve,' Alessi said, 'telling you that you've had too much wine and coming to check up on you, yet he gets to carry on exactly as he chooses…'

'Our relationship is not your concern,' Isla said, her voice shaking. There was no doubt about the sudden flare of possessiveness in Alessi's voice. 'Anyway, you flirt, you…' She tripped over her words, not quite sure of the point she was trying to make. 'You're such a chauvinist.'

'It's the Greek in me.'

They stood angry and frustrated. A kiss was there but not happening. They were back to where they had been a year ago, only the stakes were much higher now. Alessi looked at her full mouth and noticed that she ran a very pink tongue over her lips as if to tempt him.

And tempt him it did.

Isla was looking at his mouth. She was back to how she'd felt in the shower, only now Alessi was less than a step away. Her body was on fire, there was sex in the air, and when walking away might be safer, because it was Alessi, he forced the issue, voiced the truth, stated what was. 'I could kiss you now.'

Isla lifted her eyes to his and saw that the lust and the want in his matched hers. 'You could,' she invited.

She wanted his kiss. The world had disappeared and she had no thought about anything other than now and a kiss that was nearing, but she blinked at his caustic response to her provocative words.

'But I won't,' Alessi said, distaste evident in his voice. 'I happen to have respect for the person I'm with. I have no intention of getting mixed up in whatever twisted game it is that you're playing.'

Isla stepped back, felt the wall behind her and wished it would swallow her up. Alessi was right. It was twisted. The wall would not give, though, and she had to stand there and take it as Alessi continued venting, eleven months of frustration contorting his lips savagely. 'And there's another reason that I shan't kiss you—I won't give you the chance to blow me off again, Isla. You'll be the one to kiss me,' he warned. 'After you've suitably apologised.'

And with that he walked off, leaving Isla standing there, trying to think of an appropriate response to that most delicious threat.

'Never,' she called to his departing back.

'We'll see,' Alessi called, without turning around.

He was furious. He flashed a look at Rupert as he left but what angered Alessi most was that to not kiss Isla had taken all the self-control he could muster. To not press her to the wall and angrily claim her mouth had taken every ounce of his resistance.

He wasn't like that.

Yes, he might have dated an awful lot of women but he was always faithful.

This was why he ended things with Amber that night.

He wanted Isla.

He wanted her in a way he never had.

He wanted to see that snobby, derisive woman begging.

Yes, for the best part of a year he'd convinced himself otherwise but the truth remained—he wanted her.

CHAPTER FOUR

DARCIE REALLY WAS DROOPING. Once home she thanked Isla and Rupert for the night out and went straight to bed. Thankfully Isla didn't have to work out what to say—Rupert said it for her.

'I'm guessing we're breaking up?'

'We are.' Isla forced a brave smile. 'You can say that I'm sick and tired of all your other women.'

'How are you going to go at the ball with your Greek friend there? I assume he's a big part of the reason for us finishing tonight.'

'He hates me,' Isla said. 'And I don't particularly like him, either.'

'Well, that sounds like a good start to me.' Rupert smiled. He knew Isla very well and there were very few people that she allowed to get under her skin. He had felt the undeniable tension all night and had seen Alessi's eyes all too often turn to look towards Isla. 'It's more than time you got out there.'

'Well, I shan't be *getting out there* with Alessi. His relationships seem to last as long as a tube of toothpaste.'

'Ah, but you have to brush your teeth, Isla.' To Rupert, it was that simple. 'Go for it. It's as clear as anything that you fancy each other. Why not just give the two of you a try? If it doesn't work out, it's no big deal.'

It was to Isla, though.

They said goodbye at the door—it was possibly the nicest break-up in the world.

'This is way overdue, Isla,' Rupert said as he gave her a cuddle. Even he didn't know about Isabel and just how deep Isla's fears ran, and saying goodbye to her rock of ten years was hard.

'I know.' She gave him a smile. 'Will you be okay?'

'I shall, but, Isla, can I ask that you don't—'

Isla knew what he was about to say and said it for him. 'I shan't tell anyone about you.'

'Promise me.' His voice was urgent. 'I'm auditioning soon for a really big role. If I do get it then I'm going to be even more in the spotlight…' She could hear his fear and she understood it. She, too, would be terrified to have her sex life, or lack of it, put under the scrutiny of anyone, let alone having it discussed the world over. 'I haven't even told my parents, Isla…'

'It's okay,' Isla soothed, remembering the promise she had made all those years ago. 'I gave you my word.'

When Isla awoke the next morning and headed into work with Darcie, the world felt very different without her safety net.

Not that anyone could know just how exposed and vulnerable she felt. She was her usual cool self while secretly hoping that the world might treat her gently.

The world, though, had other plans for Isla—

around eleven, she answered a page from the antenatal clinic. It was Sophia, one of the community midwives, who, because of low staff numbers, was doing an extra shift on-site today and running the antenatal clinic.

'Thanks for answering so quickly,' Sophia said. 'I wasn't sure whether or not to page you. I'm probably—'

'Always page me,' Isla interrupted. 'It doesn't matter how small your concern is, I hope you know that.'

'I do,' Sophia said. 'It's not a patient I'm concerned about, more a situation that I'm not sure how to handle. Alessi dropped by this morning and said that when his sister arrived for her antenatal visit I was to page him so that he could come down. Allegra is actually his twin sister.'

'Okay,' Isla replied, wondering where this was leading as Sophia continued.

'She's thirty-two weeks gestation and Darcie has asked her to go onto a CTG monitor now for a checkup—all is well but Darcie just wanted to be thorough as she's taking over her care and Allegra has quite a complicated history. The trouble is, when I said that I would let Alessi know that she was here, Allegra asked me not to. She wants me to just say that I forgot to page him...'

'And no doubt you're worried about what Alessi will say when you tell him that you *forgot* to let him know?' Isla said, and then thought for a moment. 'It is a bit awkward,' she admitted as she pondered the issue while doing her level best to think this through as she would for any patient who was related to one of the staff here. She had to somehow forget that the staff member happened to be Alessi who, after last night, she was doing her level best to avoid.

Ignore that fact, she told herself.

'I'll come over to Antenatal now and speak with Allegra,' Isla offered. 'And I'll also deal with Alessi. Thank you for letting me know, Sophia.'

Isla made her way down to the antenatal clinic and Sophia told her where Allegra was. Isla knocked on the door and went in and smiled when she saw Allegra. She was the female version of Alessi with black eyes and black hair and, while strapped to the CTG monitor, she was also doing her level best to keep a wriggling little boy of around three years old amused.

'Hi, Allegra,' Isla greeted her. 'I'm Isla, the head of midwifery.'

'Hello, Isla.' Allegra smiled. 'Is this about Alessi? I realised as soon as I said it that the midwife was feeling a bit awkward when I asked her to pretend she'd forgotten I was here. I'm so sorry about that. I should have discussed this with Alessi myself, instead of landing my problems on Sophia.'

'It's fine,' Isla said, and looked over at the little boy. 'You've got your hands full, I see.'

'Very,' Allegra agreed. 'Sophia gave him a colouring book and some pencils but he's just climbing all over me at the moment. I think Niko's starting to fathom that he's not going to have me all to himself for much longer.'

'Probably,' Isla said, and sat down in a chair near Allegra. 'They're very intuitive and they often sense that change is about to come. Hey, Niko, do you want to come and sit with me?' Isla suggested to the little black-eyed boy who had the same curls as his uncle. 'Look what I've got…'

Niko looked at Isla, who had taken out her pen torch and was flicking it on and off. It worked as a diversion tactic almost every time with three-year-olds and thankfully it worked today. Niko climbed down from his mum's lap and made his way over to Isla. She noted that he had a slightly abnormal gait as he walked over and climbed up onto her lap.

'Look,' Isla said, flicking the pen torch on and off and then giving it to Niko, who tried to do the same. Only he soon found out that it wasn't as easy as Isla had made it look and he would hopefully take several moments to work it out and give Allegra a small break while they chatted and Allegra explained her reasons for not wanting Alessi there.

'I had a very difficult labour with Niko,' Allegra said. 'We were living in Sydney at the time. He was a breech birth and I ended up having an emergency Caesarean section after a very long labour.' Allegra paused for a moment before continuing—clearly the memory of it still distressed her. 'Niko wasn't breathing when he was born and had to be resuscitated. As a consequence he was without oxygen and has now got mild cerebral palsy.'

'That must have been a very scary time for you,' Isla offered.

'It was,' Allegra agreed. 'I wasn't at all well after the birth, either. The thing is, there were a couple of mistakes made and possibly what happened could have been prevented. I chose not to pursue it. I just wanted to put it all behind me. Alessi, though, was pretty devastated as well as furious. I know he thinks if he'd been there, or at least around, then I'd have been taken to Theatre more quickly and Niko's birth injury could have been avoided. My parents said pretty much the same to him, too.'

Isla said nothing but her heart went out to them both.

'I don't want Alessi to be involved in this birth, not because I don't think he's brilliant, it's more that if something does go wrong this time around then I don't want him blaming himself for it.'

'I completely understand that you'd feel that way.' Isla nodded but because she'd had a brief look at Allegra's notes before she'd come in, she knew that there was more. 'And?'

'And?' Allegra smiled at Isla's question.

'Is there another reason that you don't want Alessi's input?'

'There is.' Allegra rolled her eyes in the very same way that her brother did. 'I want to try and have a natural birth this time. Given what happened in my previous labour, Alessi is against the idea of trial of labour and thinks I should have a planned Caesarean section.'

'So, not only do you have to convince your obstetrician, you have to convince your brother, as well?'

'Ah, not just those two,' Allegra sighed. 'I've had to convince my husband and also my mother.' She gave a tired shake of the head. 'Usually I'm the golden one and Alessi's the black sheep but in this she thinks I should listen to him, because he's a doctor.'

Isla fought her own curiosity about that statement—while she wanted to know more about Alessi, this wasn't the place, and she could see Allegra was close to tears. 'What happened with Niko has brought up a lot of stuff for my parents. Maybe I should just have a planned Caesarean. I really am sorry for trying to involve your staff in this.'

'It's our job to be involved,' Isla said, and she truly did her best to pretend this wasn't Alessi's twin pouring her heart out to her. Which meant, if this hadn't been Alessi's twin then Isla knew exactly what she would do in this case. 'It's your pregnancy and your labour. You shouldn't go through an operation just to please your family. I can explain all that to him.'

Allegra looked dubious. 'I don't know how well he'd take it.'

'I would imagine that when I explain what's going on to Alessi, he's going to feel bad for causing you so much stress…'

'I know that he shall,' Allegra agreed. 'We're very close. The thing is Alessi has always looked out for me at school and things…' She looked at Isla. 'I remember you from school.'

Isla felt a little guilty that she didn't remember Allegra clearly.

'I got picked on a lot at school,' Allegra said. 'Well, we both did.'

'Really?' Isla couldn't imagine for a moment Alessi being picked on by anyone, he was so confident and assured, but then Allegra continued speaking.

'We were scholarship kids,' she explained. 'Which meant from the day that we started we didn't belong. At every opportunity it would be rammed down our throats that we couldn't afford to go skiing or that we didn't have the right uniform. It was very cruel. Alessi looked out for me then and is just trying to do the same now. The thing is…' Allegra hesitated and Isla stepped in.

'You don't need him to any more?'

'No, I don't.' Allegra sighed. 'I'm not going to take any risks with this baby but I really do want to try and have a natural delivery.' She thought for a long moment. 'It would be great if you could speak to him for me. I really have tried and I seem to get nowhere.'

Isla nodded. 'You're not the first patient to have this sort of problem. I've dealt with this on several occasions. No doubt I'll be the same if my sister ever gets pregnant. It's very hard to step back when you love someone, though Alessi needs to in this.'

'Thanks, Isla.'

Niko had actually fallen asleep while they'd

been talking. Isla carried him over to one of the empty reclining chairs next to Allegra and laid him down, then went and looked at the CTG monitor. 'Everything looks very good,' Isla said. 'Right, I'm going to have a word with that brother of yours and don't worry. If you have any concerns, any at all, ring through to MMU and ask to be put through to me.'

'Thanks so much.'

As she walked out of the room there was Alessi, speaking with Sophia and frowning.

'I asked you to page me as soon as Allegra arrived—'

'Alessi,' Isla said, and gave a small smile to Sophia, excusing her from the conversation. 'Sophia paged me. I need to speak with you about your sister.' She saw concern flash across his features and immediately put him at ease. 'There's nothing wrong with the baby, but before you go in and see Allegra there is something that I need to discuss with you.'

Alessi's eyebrows rose and she had a feeling he was about to walk off but he gave a small nod. 'What is it that you want to discuss?'

'Perhaps not here.' Isla gestured to one of the consulting rooms and they both walked over to it.

It was awkward to be in there with him, given all that had, or rather hadn't, taken place between them, but Isla pushed all that aside and dealt with what was important—the patient. She took a seat at the desk and Alessi did the same. With the door closed she could smell his cologne and she really wished this conversation didn't have to take place on the tail end of last night, but she had no choice in the timing of things and so she pushed on.

'I've just been speaking with Allegra. We've had quite a long conversation, in fact,' she ventured. 'The thing is, while Allegra really appreciates your concern about the pregnancy—'

'I don't need you interfering in my family, Isla,' Alessi interrupted, and it was clear that he knew what the discussion would be about and wanted no part of it.

'I'd prefer not to have to but it's not about what I'd prefer and it's not about what you need—this is about Allegra.'

Alessi took a breath. 'Isla, I'm not going to discuss this with you.'

'You don't have to discuss anything with me, Alessi,' Isla answered calmly. 'I'm just asking that you take a few minutes to listen.' He went to stand but Isla halted him. 'Alessi, Allegra isn't your patient, she's *my* patient in *my* unit.'

'I'll discuss this directly with Allegra,' Alessi said, and headed for the door.

'And cause her more stress?' Isla responded, and watched as his shoulders stiffened. It really was a difficult subject to approach. She hadn't been lying when she'd said to Allegra that she'd handled this sort of situation several times and she would be blunt if she had to be. 'Allegra knows that you're just trying to look out for her and while she does appreciate it she wants you to be the baby's uncle rather than some hovering neonatologist. Everything is going well this pregnancy.'

'Everything was going well the last one,' Alessi said, though at least he sat back down.

'Do you think that Allegra doesn't already know all that?' Isla asked, and watched as Alessi closed his eyes and breathed out. 'Do you think she hasn't wrestled for a long time with her decisions before making them?'

'I'm really causing stress for her?' he asked. When she didn't say anything his black eyes met hers and he gave a wry smile as he answered his own question. 'Clearly I am. God, I never meant to, Isla. The thing is, what happened during Niko's labour was preventable. I just want to…' His voice trailed off.

'You want to ensure that nothing goes wrong with this one,' Isla finished for him, and Alessi nodded. 'I get that but if something *does* go wrong, if an emergency does arise, do you really want to be a part of it?'

'I want to be there to ensure nothing untoward happens in the first place.'

'Look, I do get that…' Isla started but Alessi didn't let her finish.

'Allegra going for a natural delivery is a crazy idea, given what happened last time.'

'It's not a crazy idea to Allegra, and it's not a crazy idea to her obstetrician—'

'Darcie's been here all of five minutes.'

Isla chose to ignore that. She knew it was hard when another doctor took over a patient's care but it wasn't for Alessi to air his concerns to his sister so she continued with what she was saying. 'And it isn't a crazy idea to me. A lot of women want to experience a natural delivery. She'd have a closely monitored trial of labour and if things didn't progress well then, perhaps more quickly, given her history, things would move towards a Caesarean. Even if Darcie is new, our recruitment policy is vigorous and she's joined an amazing team, which means that your sister *shall* be well looked after here, Alessi, you know that.'

Alessi thought for a long moment. Really, he could only admire Isla for confronting him on this difficult subject but her help didn't end there.

'If it makes it any easier for you,' she continued, 'I'm happy to oversee Allegra's care.'

Alessi's eyes jerked up and met hers.

'Whatever you think about me personally, Alessi, however you think I landed the role, the truth is I think that we both know that I do a very good job. I will, if you would like, keep an eye on Allegra during her antenatal visits and, as far as possible, I will be there for the birth.'

'You'd do that?'

'Of course.'

Alessi was surprised by her offer but, then again, was he? For nearly a year he had chosen to believe she had got the job because of who her father was. He had been wrong about that. Alessi had known it deep down and it was confirmed right now. The patients all raved about her, there was no doubt that she ran a very good midwifery unit and now she was offering to take care of Allegra when both knew how tense things were between them. Even the fact that Allegra had discussed so much with Isla told Alessi something—she didn't open up easily to anyone, yet she had with Isla. 'I would like that and I'll back off, too,' Alessi said, and then stood. 'Thank you.'

'No problem.'

He went to go but then turned around. 'I was going to come and see you later,' Alessi said. 'But now that we're here, I might as well just say it now—I would like to apologise for the things that I said last night.' Isla found she was holding her breath as he continued, 'I had no right to lecture you about your partner and the choices you make. It was out of character for me and I really would like to apologise.'

'It's fine.'

'Also, I broke up with Amber last night, so

you don't have to worry that I'm dating one of your students.'

'Because of what I said?'

Alessi let out a very mirthless laugh. 'No.'

'But…'

'As I said, I don't cheat and, given that last night the only person I wanted was you, it seemed appropriate to end things.'

And with that he was gone and only when the door closed behind him did Isla let out the air trapped in her throat—her lungs were still closed tight.

Had he just said what he had?

Yes.

Did that mean…?

It did.

Oh, God.

It was like being tossed three flaming torches and having to learn to juggle with absolutely no clue how.

She walked out of the consulting room into a world that felt very different—Alessi liked her, in that way, and had made it clear that he was single. There was no Rupert to hide behind any more, not that she'd told Alessi that.

She was on the edge of something—scared to step off yet somehow compelled to.

Allegra was holding Niko and speaking with Sophia, but Isla watched her turn and smile widely at her brother as he came over, and as Isla approached she heard their conversation.

'You should have said.' Alessi gave her a cuddle.

'I tried,' Allegra gently scolded. 'Several times.'

'I'll back off and I'll make sure Mum and Dad do, too,' Alessi promised. 'I just…'

'I know,' Allegra said. 'I know you were just trying to do your best for us.' She looked at Isla as she joined them. 'Thank you so much, Isla.'

'It's no problem. I've spoken with Alessi and, if you're happy for me to do so, I can oversee things and come down and check all your antenatal visits, rather than your brother, and then, if you'd like, I'd be delighted to be there for your birth of your second child.'

'I'd really like that, Isla.'

'Good.'

She nodded goodbye and as Isla walked off Allegra smiled. 'I feel so much better. You really will speak to Mum and Dad?'

'Yep.'

'They'll give you a hard time,' Allegra pointed out.

'So, what's new?'

''Lessi!'' Niko, fed up with all the adults, held out his arms to his uncle and, from a slight distance Isla watched as Alessi took his little nephew in his arms and gave him a kiss and then he must have said something funny because Niko laughed and laughed and Alessi grinned, too.

Then he turned and caught her staring at him and the smile remained as she blushed and returned it then quickly walked away, to return to the ward.

Yes, she was on the edge of something.

Something temporary, though. She knew that much about Alessi and she had almost reconciled herself to that.

Yes, this year was going to be very different. Alessi was going to be her first.

Even if he mustn't know it.

Somehow she had to hold onto her glamorous, sophisticated reputation while releasing a little of her heart.

CHAPTER FIVE

DARCIE SETTLED INTO the flat and hospital amazingly well.

With one exception.

Her first week at the Victoria passed smoothly but at the start of Darcie's second week Isla heard an angry exchange coming from the treatment room and then Darcie marched out. Frowning, Isla stepped into the treatment room to find Lucas standing there, the tension still in the air and a wry smile on his face.

'Issue?' Isla checked, trying to hide her surprise because Darcie got on with everyone, and no one, no one *ever* had an issue with Lucas—he was down-to-earth and seriously gorgeous and for him to have had upset Darcie or vice versa was a surprise indeed.

'You tell me.' Lucas shrugged.

'Lucas?' Isla frowned. He was a part of the glue that tied the MMU together. He got on with everyone, was intuitive, funny and so damn good-looking that his smile could melt anyone. It would seem it simply didn't melt Darcie.

'I don't need the new obstetrician telling me I'm late and to get my act together.'

Isla let out a breath. No, that much Lucas didn't need.

'And,' Lucas drawled, 'I also don't need you to have a word for me, Isla. Whatever her issue with me is, I'll deal with it myself.'

'Fine,' Isla said, 'but whatever the hell your issues are with each other, keep them well away from the patients.'

'You know that I will.'

'I do,' Isla said. 'Let me know if you need anything…' She turned to go but Lucas halted her.

'Isla, I hate to say this, I know I was late in this morning but I really need to go home…' He blew out a breath and then went to explain but

Lucas didn't need to explain things to Isla. She knew that his home life was complicated at best and if Lucas said that he needed to go home then he was telling the truth.

'Go, then,' Isla said. 'I'll take over your patients.'

'I've only got one,' Lucas said. 'I'm expecting her to arrive any minute, I'm just setting up for her. Donna Reece, she's pretty complex.'

'You think I can't handle complex?' Isla teased.

'No, I just feel like I'm landing an awful lot on you.'

'Return the favour someday.' Isla smiled. 'Hand over the patient to me and go home.'

As Isla wheeled through the drip Lucas had set up, there was Darcie, checking drugs for the imminent arrival of Donna Reece. She was forty years old, at twenty-four weeks gestation with twins and a direct admission from the antenatal ward as she had been found to be in premature labour.

'Where's Lucas?' Darcie frowned. 'He was supposed to—'

'I've got your orders,' Isla said. 'I'm taking over this patient.'

'Oh, so he doesn't want to work with me?'

'Lucas has gone home,' Isla said. She was about to tell Darcie why and to tell her to back off Lucas, but then she remembered that Lucas had asked her not to step in. Anyway, there was no time for that. Donna was about to arrive.

'Did he page Alessi?'

'Yes,' Isla said, and as Donna was wheeled in, just the look on her face had Isla reaching for the phone to page for an anaesthetist to come directly to the delivery ward, too.

'Hi, Donna, I'm Isla...'

Isla kept her voice calm as she attached Donna to all the equipment. Things didn't look good at all and it was made worse that Donna's thirteen-year-old daughter was present and clearly distressed.

As Alessi arrived Isla was taking the young

girl down to the waiting room and she gave him a grim smile, in way of small preparation for what he was about to face.

'Have a seat in here,' Isla said to Jessica. 'I know that you've had a horrible morning...'

'I thought that Mum was just coming here for a checkup,' Jessica said. She was holding a large backpack and Isla could see a towel sticking out of it. It was the summer holidays and clearly they had intended to head out to the beach for the day after the routine appointment that had suddenly taken a different turn. 'Mum said she didn't feel well this morning and I said she'd promised we'd go out. I should have listened...'

'Jessica, I'm going to come and talk to you later. You've done nothing wrong and your mum is going to be okay.'

'But what about the babies?' Jessica asked.

'Right now the doctors are in with your mum and we'll know a lot more soon. Is there anyone I can call for you? Your dad's overseas?' Isla checked, because Lucas had told her that he was.

'He is but Mum's going to ring him and tell him to come home.'

'I'll speak to your mum and we'll see about getting someone to come and sit with you. Right now, do your best to take it easy and I'll go and see how Mum is doing.'

She went back into the delivery ward. Alessi was doing an ultrasound and his face was grim and he wasn't trying to hide it. He was clearly concerned.

'How's Jessica?' Donna asked.

'She's just worried about you and the babies,' Isla said. 'Is there anybody that you'd like me to call who can come and be with her?'

'Could you call my sister?' Donna asked. 'Tom, my husband, is in Dubai. I'm going to see what Darcie has to say and then call him and ask him to come home.' Donna closed her eyes. 'Jessica and I had an argument last night. I told her that I needed more help around the house, especially with the twins coming. Then we had another row this morning because I'd promised to take her to the beach but I told her I was too tired, when really my back was hurting and I was starting to worry that something was going wrong with the twins.' Donna started to cry. 'She said in the ambulance that she thinks this is all her fault.'

'We both know that none of this is her fault,' Isla said. 'These things happen all the time, whether there's an argument involved or not. I'll speak with your daughter at length about this,' Isla promised, and Alessi glanced up at the determined note in her voice. 'Right now, though,' Isla continued, 'we need to take care of you and your babies.'

'Darcie's said that the medicine might postpone the labour.'

'That's right,' Isla nodded, and then glanced up as Alessi came over.

'Hi, Donna.' He gave a pale smile. 'As I said, I'm going to be overseeing the twins' care.'

'Hopefully not for a while,' Donna said, but

Alessi glanced at Isla and her heart sank as Alessi continued to speak.

'I'm not sure. I have to tell you that I am very concerned about one of the twins on the ultrasound. Do you know what you're having?'

Donna nodded. 'Two boys.'

'That's right, and you know that they're not identical?'

Again Donna nodded.

'The twins are in two separate amniotic sacs and they each have their own placenta,' Alessi explained. 'The trouble is that one of the twins is smaller than the other, and the fluid around this twin…' he placed a hand high on Donna's stomach '…is significantly reduced. Most of the time our aim is to prolong the pregnancy for as long as possible but in some cases it is better that the baby is born.'

'Even at twenty-four weeks?' Donna asked, and there was a very long silence before Alessi answered.

'No,' he said gently. 'It is far too soon but this

is where it becomes a very delicate balancing game. Darcie has given you steroids that will mean that if the twins come after forty-eight hours then their lungs will be more mature than they would otherwise be. However, I'm not sure that I want the delivery to be held off for much longer. This little one needs to born soon. The placenta isn't doing its job and that twin stands a better chance out of the womb than inside.'

'But what about the other one?'

'That is why it is such a delicate balance,' Alessi said. There were no easy answers—twin A needed as long as possible inside the womb; twin B, to have a chance of survival, desperately needed to be born. The diagnosis was indeed grim. Twenty-four weeks was, in the best of cases, extremely premature but for an already small undernourished baby it didn't look good at all. Isla listened as Alessi gently led Donna down the difficult path of realisation that the babies' chances of survival were poor and that their outlook, if they did live, might not be bright.

It really was a horrible conversation to have, and he did it kindly and with compassion, but he was also clear in that he didn't offer false hope. By the end of the consultation Donna had said that she wanted everything, *everything* possible done for both twins when they were born.

'We shall,' Alessi assured her. 'Donna, I can say that you are in the very best place for this to happen. I am going to be there for your boys and I shall do all that I can for them.' He stood and looked at Isla, asking if he could have a word outside.

'Any changes, particularly to twin B, I want to be urgently paged. I've spoken to the anaesthetist and he's going to set up an epidural so that we can do an urgent section if required.'

'How long do you think twin B has got if he isn't delivered?'

'I'm hoping to buy a few days,' Alessi said. 'Though I doubt we can wait much longer than that, though that would be to the detriment of twin A, who looks very well.'

'It's a tough choice.'

'I don't think I'll have to make it.' Alessi sighed. 'She has marked funnelling,' he said, and Isla nodded. The cervix was dilated at the top end and that meant that Donna could deliver at any time.

'I'm going to go and speak with Jessica now,' Isla said, 'and then ring her aunt and ask her to come in.'

'Do you want me to speak with her?' Alessi offered, but Isla shook her head.

'I'm sure you'll be having a lot of contact with the family in the coming days and weeks. If you could just bear in mind that she's feeling guilty, when really, whether Donna was in labour or not when she presented in Antenatal, the outcome was always going to be that she was admitted today...'

'I'll keep it in mind,' Alessi said. 'Oh, and I just had a call from Allegra. She's very grateful to you. Things are much better.'

'That's good.'

'I spoke with my parents, as well, and they are doing their best now not to interfere.'

'How did that go?' Isla asked.

'Ha.' Alessi smiled. 'They do listen to me when it's about work.'

'Only then?' Isla asked, her curiosity permanently piqued when it came to Alessi, but he simply gave a small nod.

'Pretty much. I'd better get back.'

'Sure.'

'Isla?'

'Yes?'

Alessi changed his mind. 'It will keep.'

He left her smiling.

When Alessi had gone back to NICU and things were settling down with Donna, Isla had a very long chat with Jessica. Rather than speaking in her office, Isla took the young girl to the canteen and they had a drink as Isla did her best to reassure her that none of the situation was her fault.

'None of this happened because of your argument with your mum,' Isla said, when Jessica revealed her guilt. 'I promise you that. One of the twins is very small and we'd have picked up on that today at her appointment and she would have been admitted.'

'It's too soon for them to be born, isn't it?' Jessica asked.

'They're very premature,' Isla explained. 'But as I said, there's a problem with one of the twins and your mum was always going to have to deliver the twins early. Do you understand that you didn't cause this?'

'I think so,' Jessica said. 'I'm scared for my brothers.'

'I know that you are, but we're going to do all we can for them and for your mum. I've spoken with your aunt and she's on her way in and you're going to be staying with her tonight. Your mum's rung your dad and he's on his way back from Dubai.'

'It's serious, then.'

'It is,' Isla said. There was no point telling

Jessica that everything was going to be fine. It would be a lie and even with the best possible outcome, her mum and brothers were going to be at the Victoria for a very long time. 'But your mum is in the best place. Darcie, the doctor who is looking after her, is very used to dealing with difficult pregnancies. In fact, she's just come over from England and we're thrilled to have her expertise, and Alessi, the doctor who will be in charge of your brothers' care, is one of the best in his field. He'll give them every chance.'

She let the news sink in for a moment. It was a hard conversation, but Isla knew that it might be easier on Donna if she prepared Jessica and ultimately easier on Jessica to be carefully told the truth. 'Why don't we get Mum a drink and take it up to her now?'

Jessica nodded and they headed back up to the ward. Isla was pleased to see Jessica and Donna have a cuddle and Donna reiterate to Jessica that none of this was her fault.

It was a long day and it didn't end there because just as Isla was about to head for her home she got an alert on her computer that it was her fortnightly TMTB group tonight.

'I completely forgot,' Isla groaned to Emily. 'I honestly thought it was next week.'

'Do you want me to take it?' Emily offered. 'I can go home for an hour and then come back.'

'That's lovely of you but, no, it's fine.' Isla smiled. She knew how stretched Emily was and it was incredibly generous of her to offer to stay back.

Isla did some paperwork to fill in the time and then headed over to the room they used for TMTB. She turned on the urn and put out a couple of plates of biscuits and set up. Usually there were five to ten young mums, all at various stages of pregnancy.

As Isla was setting up a young girl put her head around the door. She was clearly nervous and Isla gave her a warm smile.

'Are you looking for Teenage Mums-To-Be?' Isla asked, and the girl gave a tentative nod.

'Then you're in the right place. I'm Isla.'

'Ruby.'

'I'm just setting up but come in and help yourself to a drink. The rest of the group should start arriving any time now.'

Isla watched as the young girl came in. She was incredibly slim and, Isla guessed, around sixteen years old. She was wearing shorts and a large T-shirt and if she hadn't been here, Isla wouldn't have guessed that she was pregnant. It was good that she was here so early in her pregnancy, Isla thought, but when she looked over to where Ruby was making a drink her heart sank as she saw the young girl slipping a few biscuits into her pocket and then a few more.

She was hungry, Isla realised.

Pregnant and hungry.

'I'll be back in a moment, Ruby,' Isla said, and headed back to the ward. In her office Isla rang down to Catering and asked for sandwiches and a fruit platter and some jugs of juice to be sent up. There were some perks to being a manager because her request went through unquestioned and Isla only wished that she had thought of this long ago. Still, TMTB was a relatively new project and they were all still feeling their way.

Gradually the other girls started to arrive and at seven the group started and introductions were made. Harriet was nineteen and this was her first pregnancy. She had already been told that her baby was going to have significant issues.

'He's going to have to have an operation as soon as he's born,' Harriet said. 'I don't really understand what is happening, but Mum said that she'll come to my next appointment with me.'

'That's good,' Isla said. 'It's really helpful to have someone with you at these appointments because sometimes you can forget to ask a question or later not remember what was said.'

Then it was Alison's turn. She was about four weeks away from her delivery date and very excited. 'I didn't even want to be pregnant,' Alison admitted, 'and now I can't wait.'

Isla smiled. This was one of the reasons that she loved this group so much. It was very helpful for others to realise that the conflicting emotions they might be feeling weren't reserved for them. Here the girls got to share in each other's journeys and Isla had seen that Ruby was listening intently, though she was guarded when it was her turn to speak.

'I'm Ruby,' she said. 'I'm fourteen weeks pregnant.'

'How old are you, Ruby?' Isla asked, and suspicious eyes looked back at her before she answered the question.

'Seventeen.' She was immediately defensive. 'My mum wanted me to have an abortion but I'm not getting rid of it.'

'How are things with you and Mum at the moment?' Isla gently pushed, and Ruby shrugged.

'I haven't really seen much of her. I'm staying with friends at the moment.' Isla made a mental note to look at Ruby's file and see if there was anything more that she could do to support her during this difficult time. She would talk to her away from the group, Isla decided, but for now she moved on.

Alison had some questions about delivery and pain control and said that she didn't want to stay in bed.

'You don't have to,' Isla said. 'We usually encourage mothers to move around during labour—walking around is wonderful.'

There were always a lot of questions. Isla loved the enthusiasm of the teenage mums and more often than not both the questions and answers were interspersed with a lot of laughter.

It was that sound of laughter that alerted Alessi as he walked out of Maternity, having just checked in again on Donna.

He hadn't stopped all day and seeing a huge trolley laden with food being delivered to the room, he assumed that there was an administration meeting going on.

He was starving and, completely shameless, he followed the trolley into the room, to be greeted by a sight that he wasn't expecting!

Isla felt awkward around Alessi and possibly she had every reason to now as he put his head around the door just in time to capture her in a deep squat on the floor as she showed the girls how that position opened up the pelvis nicely!

Here, though, was not the place to be awkward and so, instead of hurriedly standing, as was her instinct, she remained in a rather embarrassing position and gave him a very bright smile as the girls turned round to see who had interrupted the group.

'Did you smell the food, Alessi?' Isla asked.

'I did.' Alessi grinned. 'Sorry to disturb you. I thought it might be a work meeting and I could steal a few sandwiches. I'll let you guys get on.'

'Shall we feed him?' Isla said to the girls, and they all agreed that they should. Well, of course they did—Alessi was seriously gorgeous. He went over to the trolley and as he selected some sandwiches and fruit Isla introduced him.

'Alessi is one of our neonatologists. Some of you may have quite a bit to do with him once your baby is here.'

He gave a small wave but instead of taking his food and walking off he turned to the group. 'For feeding me you can ask any questions that you want.'

Isla was more than pleasantly surprised and, yes, the girls, especially Harriet, did have questions that they wanted to ask, and Isla knew she had lost her audience.

'Why don't we all get something to eat?' Isla suggested, and before she'd even finished the sentence chairs were scraping as the girls headed over for supper and to talk to the gorgeous doctor who had joined them.

She was going to provide food each time, Isla decided, watching as Ruby and another young mum really did fill up their plates. They were hungry, seriously hungry, Isla realised, kicking herself that she hadn't thought to do this before.

Well, that would change now.

'We'll have pizza next time,' Isla said, and she saw Ruby's ears prick up. Anything that brought these young mums back to the group was more than worth it. Not only did their questions get answered but through meeting regularly friendships were forged, and it also meant that Isla could keep an extra eye on these vulnerable young girls.

Alessi was really fantastic with them, answering Harriet's questions easily. 'Do you want me to come again?' Alessi asked Isla. 'I could prepare a talk if you like.'

'That would be great,' Isla said. 'We meet each fortnight.'

Alessi pulled out his phone and checked his calendar. 'I already have a meeting scheduled for the next one and the fortnight after that is my parents' wedding anniversary…' He thought for a moment. 'What time does it finish?'

'About eight thirty or nine,' Isla said.

'That's fine, then,' Alessi said, then turned to the group. 'Think up some questions for me.' He smiled at Harriet and then said goodbye to them and left. There were a few wolf whistles as he went and Isla laughed, glad to see the lift to the group that Alessi had given.

And also terribly aware of the lift in her.

After she finished up, instead of heading straight for home Isla went up to the ward.

She guessed he'd be there and she was right.

'Aren't you finished?' Isla asked.

'I'm staying tonight,' Alessi said.

'You're not on call.'

'Tell that to the twins.'

'Thanks for offering to come and speak. It will be good.'

'No problem,' Alessi said. 'They seem a nice group. Truth be told, I admire them.'

'I do, too,' Isla said, and turned to go.

'Isla?'

'Yes?'

This time he didn't tell her that whatever he had to say would keep. 'Are you ready for Saturday?' Alessi asked.

'Saturday?' Isla frowned. 'Oh, yes, the ball. I'd forgotten.'

'You attend so many things, I'm not surprised that it slipped your mind.'

It hadn't slipped her mind. It was just that she had been so focused on Donna that for a little while she had managed to push aside the fact it was the ball on Saturday.

She had seen the seating plans and would be sitting between her father and Alessi. Both were there to represent the maternity and neonatal units. She was excited, nervous and never more so than when she looked into his eyes, and Alessi touched on a necessary topic if things were going to proceed.

'I promise I'll behave this time if Rupert is there.' Even saying his name, even thinking of being there with Isla and him made Alessi's skin crawl, but he did his best not to show it as he broached the sensitive subject.

'Rupert's not going.'

'Oh,' Alessi said. 'Is he back in the States?'

'I think so.'

'Think so?'

Jump, Isla told herself, but her legs were shaking and she wanted to turn and run, not that Alessi could tell. As coolly as she would face the guests on Saturday, as easily as she delivered a speech, even if she was shaking inside, Isla somehow met his gaze as she took that dangerous leap.

'We broke up.'

'Oh.' Alessi had to concentrate on not letting out a sigh of relief. 'I'm sorry,' he said, just as Isla had said to him on the night they had met.

'I'm not,' Isla said, just as Alessi had once said to her.

She watched as his lips stretched into a smile, and either every baby on the delivery ward simultaneously stopped crying and every conversation had suddenly halted, or the world simply stopped for a moment. Whichever it was, it was irrelevant to them as silence invaded and realisation dawned on them both—Saturday night was theirs to look forward to.

CHAPTER SIX

ISLA HAD TRIED to speak with Ruby at the end of the TMTB meeting but she hadn't been able to get very far. Ruby had merely shrugged in answer to Isla's questions and given her a look that only teenagers could, a look that said, *what would you know?*

After the group there had been loads of sandwiches left over and a couple of the girls, Ruby included, had taken up Isla's suggestion to help themselves as it would only be thrown out, but when Isla had tried to speak with her Ruby had said that she had to go.

Isla didn't mind being snubbed. She was just very glad that Ruby had turned up and hoped that the promise of pizza might lure her back, if nothing else, and she dropped in on handover the following morning to tell her team the same.

'If I'm not there and one of you is taking the TMTB group, either ring down to Catering or get some pizza delivered,' Isla said.

'Can we bring in a cake?' Emily asked, and Isla smiled. Trust Emily to want to do more.

'No, Emily, you've already got more than enough on your plate without feeding hungry teenagers.' Isla shook her head. 'There's room in the TMTB budget to ring for pizza or to order from Catering. I do want to have a think about it, though. I can't stand the idea that these girls might be hungry...'

A bell buzzed and Isla gave her staff a smile. 'I'll get it. You carry on with handover.' But as she walked out of the staffroom the bell buzzed again and Isla quickly crossed the ward, her heart galloping when she saw that it was coming from Donna and that it must be urgent because she wasn't taking her finger off the bell.

Flick, one of the midwifery students, was, in fact, the one who was pressing the bell.

'Well done,' Isla said, because as soon as Isla appeared Flick moved to open a delivery pack.

'They're coming...' Donna sobbed.

'It's okay,' Isla said, pulling on gloves and giving instructions to Emily, who on hearing the urgency of the buzzer had followed Isla in. 'Fast-page Darcie and the neonatal crash team.'

'I wanted Tom to be here...' Donna sobbed.

'His flight gets in this morning, doesn't it?' Isla asked, and Donna went to answer but nature got in first.

'Something's coming...' Donna said, and Isla recognised the fear in Donna's voice, not just professionally but personally, too, and, just as she had that night with Isabel, she stayed calm.

At least now she knew what to do professionally.

'It's okay,' Isla said. 'We're ready for them.'

They were ready, almost. Staff were busy plugging in two Resuscitaires in the side room that

Donna had been allocated. Isla could hear footsteps running along the corridor and was grateful for the sound for indeed a baby was coming.

'Don't push, Donna,' Isla said as she felt the baby's little head. 'I know that you want to, but let's just try and slow this down a little.'

Isla wanted to slow things down, not just to minimise any trauma to the tiny baby's brain but also to ensure there were plenty of staff and equipment ready when this baby made its rapid entrance into the world. Isla met Donna's gaze. 'Just breathe,' Isla said, and a petrified Donna nodded, using all her power to give her baby a few more vital seconds inside her.

Alessi came in then. He was a bit out of breath from running and his hair was soaking and his scrubs were damp—clearly he had been in the shower when his pager had gone off. He stood, watching, but even with Donna doing her best not to push, the next contraction saw the baby delivered into Isla's hands.

He was tiny but vigorous and very red. He let

out a small cry as Alessi quickly cut the cord, took the tiny bundle from Isla and carried him over to the resuscitation table.

'Twin A,' Isla said to Darcie, who was running in. 'Born at seven forty-eight.'

'So we're waiting on twin B,' Darcie said to Donna, who lay back on her pillow and started to cry. Isla glanced over to the Resuscitaire where Alessi was concentrating hard, and so, too, were the rest of the team.

'What's happening?' Donna asked. There was a huge crowd around the cot but it was all very calm and controlled.

'Looking beautiful!' came Alessi's strong voice. 'He is moving and fighting me, Donna, but I have put down a tube to give him some medicine to his lungs, that's why you can't hear him crying. Do you have a name?'

'Elijah.'

There was a flurry of activity and Isla looked over as the staff started to prepare to move the baby over to NICU. Then Alessi came over and spoke with Donna. 'He's doing as well as can be expected,' Alessi said. 'We are going to get Elijah over to NICU now, where they are ready for him.'

'Can I see him?'

'Briefly,' Alessi said. 'Later you will have more time with Elijah but we want him over there now.'

The incubator was wheeled over but Donna's brief time with her son was soon thwarted as she first folded over and then lay back on the bed. The second twin was coming and Alessi nodded to his team to take the baby up to NICU as Darcie took over the second delivery.

'Cord's around the neck,' Darcie said. 'Very friable…' The umbilical cord was so thin and weak that it tore as Darcie tried to loop it over the baby's head but already the tiny baby was slipping out.

When Isla saw him delivered she was holding her breath, even as she clamped the severed cord. She never made comparisons—in fact Isla did everything she could not to think of that awful night with Isabel whenever a baby was born.

She couldn't help but compare this morning, though.

He was so tiny and his arms and legs were spindly and his little eyes were fused closed. The difference was that this little one started to put up a fight. Even as Darcie lifted him and handed him straight to a neonatal nurse his arms were flailing and he let out a tiny mewing cry as the nurse took him over to Alessi.

'Let me hold him,' Donna called out. 'Alessi, I want to hold him.'

Alessi didn't say anything at that point, at least not to Donna. Instead, he spoke to the little boy.

'Hello, beautiful baby,' he said, and Isla felt tears prick at the backs of her eyes as Alessi did his best to shut out Donna's pleas to hold her baby and instead did everything he could to give this little life a chance. 'Do you have a name for your son?' Alessi asked.

'Archie,' Donna said, and then lay back on the pillow, exhausted and defeated, aching to hold her son but knowing he needed the skill of the medical team now.

Isla did her best to comfort Donna as the team worked on. There was no way to see what was happening. Alessi, the anaesthetist and two neonatal nurses were around the resuscitation cot. They could hear the baby's fast heart rate on the monitor and Alessi issuing instructions. The mood was markedly more urgent than it had been for Elijah, and Donna started to cry.

'I just want to hold him,' Donna said to Isla.

'I know you do,' Isla said. 'But right now he needs to be with the medical team—they're doing everything they can for him.'

It was an interminable wait, made all the more difficult because Donna's husband called to say that he had landed. When Donna couldn't speak Isla took over the call and Alessi glanced up at the calmness in her voice as she introduced herself to the distraught husband.

'Tom, Donna is exhausted and upset but we're taking care of her. Elijah was born first and has been taken up to the neonatal intensive care unit, and Archie...' she glanced over and met Alessi's sombre gaze '...is being worked on by the team now. We hope to get him up to the intensive care unit soon.' She took a breath. 'Have you cleared customs? Good, go over to the information desk and explain what's happening and hopefully they can see you to the front of the taxi queue.' There was another pause. 'They're very premature, Tom. Right now the team are doing their best for your sons.'

It wasn't an easy call but somehow she did her best not to scare Tom while still conveying the need for him to get there urgently because it was clear that Archie especially was struggling. That was confirmed when Alessi came over and spoke to Donna, his expression grim. 'Donna, I am very concerned for Archie. I want to move him up to NICU where we can do some more tests on him and where there is more equipment…'

'I want to hold him.'

'I know you do,' Alessi said, 'but we are not at that stage—Archie is fighting and I will do everything I can to assist him in that. For now we'll bring him over so you can have a little look at him. He's very beautiful…'

The incubator was wheeled over. Archie looked like a little washed-up frog, but Alessi was right—he was a very beautiful baby. 'Put your hand in,' Alessi said, and Donna did, stroking his little cheek and then holding his fingers. 'I'm going to take him up. I also want to see how his brother is doing. As soon as I can I'll come and speak with you or I'll send someone else if I am busy with them.'

'Thank you. If something happens…' Donna couldn't say it but Alessi did.

'If either of the twins takes a turn for the worse you will be told, Donna, and the staff here will do everything they can to get you to your babies. Right now, though, I need to get him to NICU.'

'Mummy loves you,' Donna said, and Isla felt her heart twist, and for once she was struggling to keep up her cool mask. She wanted to go over to Alessi, to tell him to just give Donna her baby, to accept the inevitable and give them this precious time.

It wasn't her place to, though. Donna had made it clear before the twins' birth that she wanted everything possible done for her sons. It was for Isla to support that decision now.

It was a long and difficult day. Isla went through the birth with Flick and all that had happened. Donna's husband arrived and he went up to NICU. Though Donna ached to go and see her twins she had a small bleed after delivery and wasn't well enough to go up till much later in the day.

Isla went with her.

First they saw Elijah, the tiny, though relatively bigger, twin. 'It seems impossible…' Donna said, and Isla just stood back and let her have the time with her son. She looked over to the next cot and Alessi was there and caught her eyes, his expression still grim.

When Isla took Donna over she knew why.

Donna completely broke down when she saw her little man hooked up to so many machines.

'He's not well enough to be held,' Alessi said. 'Just talk to him, he'll know your voice.'

Alessi, Isla noted, looked exhausted. He was also incredibly patient and kind. For close to a year she had dismissed him as some sort of killer flirt and had avoided him at all costs.

Now there was no avoiding him.

On Friday, at the end of a long shift, at the end of a very long week, she walked into her office to find Alessi sitting there with Jessica, the twins' older sister.

'Excuse me.' Alessi glanced up as she came in. 'I was just speaking with Donna, and Jessica asked if she could have a word. I just came to the nearest room.'

'That's fine.' Isla smiled. 'I'll leave you to it.'

'No, don't go,' Alessi said. 'Jessica was just telling me that she's too nervous to see the twins but that her mother thinks that she should.'

'Do you want to see them?' Isla asked.

'I don't know,' Jessica admitted. 'I've seen their photos and there are so many machines.'

'NICU can be a scary place,' Isla said. 'Alessi is actually coming to speak to my Teenage Mums-To-Be group, in a few weeks' time, to prepare them in case their babies have to go there. It can be a bit overwhelming but once you get past the machines you'll see your brothers.'

'That is what I was just telling Jessica,' Alessi agreed. 'They are very cute. Elijah is very much the big brother. Stoic and very strong, he doesn't like to cry or make a fuss…'

'And Archie?' Jessica asked, and Isla heard the twist in the young girl's voice.

'He's way too cute,' Alessi said, and Isla smiled at the genuine warmth in his voice as he went on to tell Jessica about her youngest brother. 'His eyes have just opened and he loves the sound of voices, he really does calm down when he hears someone say his name.'

'I used to talk to him when Mum was pregnant,' Jessica said.

'Then he would know your voice.' Alessi smiled but then looked over when Isla's cool voice broke in.

'Are you scared to love them, Jessica?' she asked, and Alessi could only blink in surprise. Isla asked the tough questions and had clearly got straight to the difficult point because Jessica nodded and started crying. 'I'm guessing you already do love them,' Isla said.

'They might die, though.'

'I know,' Isla said. 'And I know that is so hard to even begin to deal with, but whatever is going to happen you can still have some time with them and let yourself be their big sister. Would you like me to come and spend some time with them with you?'

Clearly it was what Jessica did want because

half an hour later, instead of collapsing on the sofa and being grateful that it was the start of Friday night and the end of a long week, Isla was up on NICU with Jessica.

There was no place she would rather be, though. Watching as Jessica's fear was replaced by smiles, seeing little Archie's eyes flicker and possibly, possibly a hint of a smile on his lips was time well spent indeed. They took photos and Jessica let her friends know all about her two brothers via social media.

'I'm off.' Alessi stood by the incubator. He had changed out of scrubs and was wearing black jeans and a gunmetal-grey top and he looked like the man who had made her heart flip over on sight all those months ago. 'I'll see you tomorrow,' he said to Isla.

'There's a big ball tomorrow night,' Isla explained to Jessica. 'Alessi's getting an award.'

'And I'll see you on Monday,' he said to little Archie. 'In the meantime, behave.' He nodded his head in the direction of the corridor and Isla excused herself from Jessica, who was holding her brother's tiny hand. 'It's good she's had some time with them.'

'I know.' Isla smiled. 'It's going to be tough on her. How do you think Archie—'

'It's minute by minute,' Alessi interrupted, the inevitable answer because there were no guarantees in NICU and especially not with a baby who was so fragile and small. 'Just take the good times, that's all you can do sometimes. Are you off now?'

Isla paused before answering; she had a feeling, more than a feeling that they were on the edge of something. That if she said yes, then she'd be joining him for dinner tonight, or for drinks, or for…

Isla looked into his black eyes and there was an absence of fear. Yes, she knew, given his reputation, it could only ever be fleeting. She knew, too, that she couldn't tell him her truth—he would surely run a mile—yet she knew she was ready.

For him.

Yet, while she wanted to say yes, some things came first. 'I think I'm going to be here for as long as Jessica wants me to be.'

'Fair enough.' Alessi smiled. 'I'll see you tomorrow, then.'

'You shall.'

'Funny, but I'm actually looking forward to it now.'

She knew what he meant and her answer told him the same. 'So am I.'

CHAPTER SEVEN

ISLA WASN'T FEELING quite so brave the next morning, though there was still a flutter of anticipation in her stomach for the coming night as she downed a grapefruit juice before heading into work for a couple of hours.

'Haven't you got a ball that you're supposed to be getting ready for?' Darcie teased as they headed out the door.

'I'm getting my hair done at two,' Isla said.

'I guess you've got this type of thing down to an art. Still, if I were going to a ball instead of working this weekend, I'd need more than a hair appointment to get me ball-ready! What are you wearing?'

'Black,' Isla said. 'Or red, I haven't decided. All I know is that I've got a mountain in my inbox that needs to be scaled. The weekends when I'm not officially there are the only times I can get anything done on the paperwork front.'

Instead of taking the tram, they walked. Darcie wasn't on until nine and Isla wasn't officially working anyway, so they took their time, enjoying the morning and stopping at Isla's favourite café. She picked up a coffee and a pastry to have at her desk and Darcie did the same.

'I love the food here,' Darcie groaned. She'd really taken to the café culture of Melbourne and Isla was only too happy to show her her favourite haunts. Once on the MMU, Darcie took her breakfast to the staffroom to get handover from Sean, and instead of saying hi to the staff Isla headed straight for the quiet of her office. She was just unlocking the door when she saw Alessi walking down the corridor.

'I thought you were off this weekend?' Isla frowned.

'Not any more—I got called in at four,' Alessi

said. 'I've just been speaking with Donna and her husband.'

He followed her into the office. 'Archie had a large cerebral haemorrhage overnight. We're taking down all the equipment and letting nature take its course. Emily is about to take them up to NICU to have some time with him.'

'Oh, poor Donna…'

'Poor Archie,' Alessi said. 'He's such a fighter…' And then, to Isla's surprise, Alessi cried. Not a lot, but he'd been tired already and being called in at four to find hope had gone and sharing the news with Archie's loving family all caught up with him and Alessi did let out a couple of tears.

Isla just stood there, more than a touch frozen. She wasn't very good with her own emotions, let alone dealing with Alessi's, and her lack of response didn't go unnoticed.

'You're much kinder to your patients when they're upset,' Alessi pointed out, and gave a wry smile as he gathered himself back together as Isla still stood there.

She could cope when it was a patient; she could survive only by staying a step back. Alessi made her want to take that step forward but she just didn't know how.

'I just hate it that he had everything stacked against him. Had he been a girl he'd have been stronger,' Alessi said. 'Or had it been a single pregnancy at twenty-four weeks…even if he'd been the first to be born, he'd have had more of a chance, but everything that could go wrong went wrong for him.'

'Maybe he's getting to you because he's a twin, too…' Isla offered.

'They all get to me,' Alessi said. 'Though Archie has more than most—he really did want to live.' He looked at Isla. Was it exhaustion that made him be honest, or was it simply that it was her? 'I'm not actually a twin. I was the second born of triplets, with Allegra the last.

My brother was the firstborn and died when he was five days old.'

The same age as Archie.

'Is that why you're so driven?' Isla asked.

'Oh, I'm driven now, am I?' Alessi teased. 'Last week you were warning me away from your staff.'

'It would seem you're both.'

Alessi shrugged. 'I guess. You feel you have to make up for all the opportunities that they never had.'

She remembered the black-sheep comment that Allegra had made about Alessi, and curiosity got the better of her now for she wanted to know more about him. 'Did your parents push you?'

Alessi nodded. 'You know, apparently, Geo, my brother, would never have spoken back to them. In fact, he'd be married by now and would have given them grandchildren.'

Isla smiled.

'And he wouldn't have given up piano at fifteen or…' Alessi shook his head. Things were moving closer to a painful part of his past than he would like, so he wrapped it up there. 'The list goes on. I really feel for Elijah, too. If he makes it.'

She watched as Alessi yawned. She could see he was exhausted and if it were any of her staff Isla would have told them to go home.

'Shouldn't you let Jed take over Archie's care?' Isla ventured, referring to the neonatologist on this weekend. 'You've been here all week and you've got a big night tonight. Surely you need—'

'What I *need*,' Alessi interrupted, 'are three things from you.'

'Three things?'

'Your coffee and whatever smells good in that bag…'

'What's the third?' Isla said, handing them over.

'If I don't get there tonight, can you give my speech for me?'

'Alessi, you're up for an award, I think it's taken as a given that you'll be there. My father—'

'Archie is having seizures,' Alessi interrupted. 'Violent ones, and they aren't nice for his family to see. Jessica wants to be there also and I want his death to be as gentle and as pain-free as possible. I want to be there for him. I'm sorry if it upsets your father that I might not make it but right now Archie is my priority.'

Alessi waited. He knew she was about to protest and he actually wanted her to. *That* was his tipping point. When anyone tried to come between him and his work Alessi walked away very easily. He wanted not to get in too deep; he wanted her to insist that he be there tonight.

Instead, she nodded her assent.

'Fine,' she said, though her father would think it anything but fine if Alessi didn't show up. 'What do you want me to say on your behalf?'

'Whatever is said at such things. I'm sure you'll give an excellent speech,' Alessi said.

'That sounds like an insult.'

It was, actually. He looked at her, so completely calm and unruffled, even as he had broken down, and knew she'd be the same tonight. 'Do any of them get to you?'

'Sorry?'

'I remember the night we met. You were all animated, completely enthralled about a baby that had just been delivered.' He watched her cheeks redden and rather than leave things there he chose to pursue them. 'I've seen you elated but I've never seen you upset and, though avoiding each other, we've still found ourselves working together at times.'

'When have I avoided you?'

'Come off it, Isla,' Alessi said. 'And don't avoid the question. Do any of them get to you?'

'I don't let them get to me,' Isla said, hopefully slamming the door closed on that observation, but Alessi wrenched it straight back open.

'That would take an awful lot of self-control.'

'Not really.' She tried to keep her voice even.

'Yes, really. Otherwise it would mean that you're completely burnt out and I don't believe that you are.'

'You don't know me,' Isla said.

'I know that I don't, because a year ago I could have sworn that we were getting on, that we were enjoying each other's company, that you wanted me as much as I wanted you,' he said. 'Yet it would seem I was wrong.'

Isla wanted to tear her eyes from his but somehow she made herself hold his gaze.

'I may be wrong now,' Alessi said, and Isla knew that she could turn and head to her desk and he would go, but she didn't. Instead, she stood there as he continued speaking, the air between them crackling with tension. 'The thing is, I won't put myself in that position again. You'll never give me that look again, Isla...'

She wanted to point out that she wasn't giving him *that* look now; she wanted to point out that she wasn't turning and walking off. The air seemed too thick for her lungs and Isla's eyes flicked to his mouth, to his soft, full lips, and she wanted to place hers there, or for his mouth to move to hers, but Alessi just stood his ground.

'When you're ready to apologise for that night…'

'Apologise?' Isla gave an incredulous smile.

Alessi didn't return the smile. 'Yes, apologise,' he confirmed. 'The next move is yours.'

'I'm not with you.'

'You'll kiss me, Isla.'

'And if I don't?'

'Then we both die wondering.'

She would, Isla realised.

No matter what the future held, if a part of it did not contain a night with Alessi, then she would die wondering because he was possibly the most beautiful, sensual man to cross her path and, yes, she wanted her time with him, for however long they had.

'I need to go,' Alessi said. 'Thank you for the coffee.'

'I hope today goes better than expected for you,' Isla croaked.

'It won't,' Alessi said, 'but some things have to be faced and dealt with.' He turned and opened the office door.

Her face was on fire, his words playing over and over.

Some things had to be dealt with and faced, but not this.

Alessi's invitation turned fears into pleasure.

CHAPTER EIGHT

DARCIE HAD PROVED to be a brilliant flatmate but as Isla got ready for the ball she was actually relieved to have the place to herself.

Nothing was going to happen between her and Alessi tonight, she told herself, except Isla knew where their kiss could lead.

She'd fought it once after all.

Isla got back from the hairdresser's at four, where she'd had her thick blonde hair curled and pinned up and had also had her nails done in a neutral shade as she still hadn't decided what to wear tonight.

Red, Isla thought, taking out her dress and holding it up, yet it was everything she wasn't—it was bold, confident and sexy, and Alessi could possibly sue her under the Trade Descriptions Act once he got the dress off!

Black.

Safe.

Only it felt far from safe when she put it on. It showed her cleavage, it showed the paleness of her skin and the flush in her cheeks whenever his name came to mind, which it did at regular fifteen-second intervals.

He might not even be there, Isla reminded herself. Except that thought didn't come as a relief.

She could still feel the heat between them from that morning. Her body, as she dressed for the night, acutely recalled the burn of his gaze and the delicious warning that the next move was hers. There had been no physical contact that morning yet it felt as if there had been.

Isla was shaking as she put on her make-up, shaking with want, with nerves, with the absolute shock of the availability of Alessi should she choose to make a move.

Should she choose?

Isla looked at herself in the mirror and realised she already had.

She wanted Alessi.

A car had been arranged—Charles Delamere didn't want his daughter arriving in a taxi—and Isla sat in the back, staring ahead. The sights of Melbourne were familiar; the feeling inside wasn't. There was no Isabel to chat with, no Rupert to deflect male attention.

She stepped into the venue alone.

Her eyes scanned the reception room as she drank champagne and sparkled as she was expected to.

There was no sign of him.

Relief and disappointment mingled as they were called to take their seats.

'Where's Manos?' Charles frowned at the empty seat at the table.

'I think that he may be stuck at the hospital,' Isla said. 'He's asked me to make a speech on his behalf if he can't get here.'

'You are joking?' Charles snapped. 'The whole point of this award is to raise NICU's profile. How are we going to get people signing cheques if the star of the show can't even be bothered to turn up?'

'Dad.' Isla looked at him. 'He's with a family—'

'Isla,' her father broke in. 'To be able to take care of the *families*, sometimes you have to look at the bigger picture. I told him the same when I had lunch with him the other day. Not that he wanted to hear it. He's an arrogant…' Charles's voice trailed off as Alessi approached the table but then he stood and shook Alessi's hand.

'Good to see that you *finally* made it,' Charles said. 'I thought I'd clearly outlined how important tonight was.'

'You did.' Alessi pushed out a smile but didn't elaborate or explain the reason for his lateness. He looked like heaven in a tux, but he'd clearly rushed. His hair was damp and he hadn't shaved, which somehow he got away with. There was a teeny stand-off between the two men and Isla found herself holding her breath, though why she didn't know.

Alessi took a seat beside her and the fragrance of him, the scent of him, the warmth of him was the reason Isla turned. Greeting the guest, manners, polite conversation had nothing to do with the turn of her head.

'How was today?'

'I've had better,' Alessi responded. 'I'm pretty wrecked. I don't want to talk about it here.' He wasn't in the mood for conversation. It had been a hell of a day and it had depleted him, and he didn't need Isla's coolness, neither did he need Charles's sniping.

'I'm sorry,' Isla said, and he glanced over and those two words and their gentle delivery helped.

'It was peaceful.' Alessi conceded more information. 'I'm glad that I stayed.' He couldn't think about it right now so he looked more closely at Isla, who was a very nice distraction from dark thoughts, and the night seemed a little brighter.

'You look amazing.'

'Thanks.' Isla smiled. 'So do you.'

They shared a look for a moment too long. She could have, had there been no one else present, simply reached over and kissed him. It was there, it just was, and Alessi knew it, too, and he confirmed it with words.

'You have to say sorry first.'

Isla just laughed. There was a thrill in her spine and all the nerves of today, of yesteryear just blew away. It should be just them but the entrée was being placed in front of her.

'I'm going to have to disappear,' Alessi said, 'and write my speech. I didn't get a chance today.'

'I've already written it,' Isla said, and handed him a piece of paper. 'Just lose the first part.'

'The first part?'

'"Dr Manos regrets that he's unable to be here tonight."'

'Dr Manos is suddenly very glad that he is.' Alessi smiled. It was a genuine smile and one that had seemed a long way off when he had left the hospital. Had it not been for this commitment, tonight would have been spent alone. Alessi took each death very personally and had long since found out that a night on the town or casual sex did nothing to fill up the black hole he climbed into when a little life was lost.

His grief was still there yet her smile did not dismiss it and neither did his.

Isla could hear her father asking a question, breaking the spell, dragging them back to the table, to the ball, to the world.

Dinner was long, the speeches even longer, and Alessi noted that Isla chatted easily with the guests at the table during dinner and listened attentively to the speeches.

She really was enjoying herself. Alessi shared her humour. His foot pressed into her calf on one occasion, not suggestively, more to share an unseen smile when one of the recipient's speeches went on and on and on.

Then it was Alessi's turn to take to the stage.

Charles gave a rather long-winded introduction about the work he had done in the year that Alessi had been at the Victoria and how pleased they were to have such talent on board.

Isla watched as Alessi went up to the stage, the speech she had written in his hand, and he took a moment to arrange the microphone. Absolutely she could see why it was her father wanted a more visible profile for Alessi because, even before he had spoken, he held the room.

She watched him glance down at his speech and, yes, he omitted the first part where Isla had explained that, regretfully, he couldn't be there.

He thanked everyone present and then Isla froze as Alessi hesitated and she realised she had omitted to mention a small joke she had written—*I'd especially like to thank the extraordinary Isla Delamere for her amazing work on the MMU*. It would have been funny had *she* read it out. Instead, Alessi's face broke into a smile and he met her gaze.

She could feel her father's impatience at the

small lull in proceedings, she could feel her own lips stretching into a smile as Alessi omitted her joke and then moved on.

"'I am very proud to receive this award,'" Alessi said, reading from Isla's notes. "'But more than that, I am incredibly grateful to work alongside skilled colleagues at such a well-equipped hospital. It helps when you can say, in all honesty, to parents that everything possible is being done or was done. It makes impossible decisions and difficult days somewhat easier to be reconciled to.'"

It was the truth, Alessi thought.

That Archie had been given every chance had been a huge source of comfort to Donna. That the facilities were top class, that there had been a private area for the family to take their necessary time with empathetic staff discreetly present had made his passing more bearable.

He wrapped up the speech and then added a line of his own, or rather he didn't completely omit Isla's.

'I would especially like to thank Isla Delamere for being here tonight and for her amazing work on the MMU.'

Ouch!

Isla was blushing as Alessi returned to his seat.

'Thank you,' Alessi said. Her words had hit home. Yes, he might loathe this side of things but he was starting to accept that it might be necessary. No, he wouldn't be appearing on morning television, as Charles had in mind for him, but he would make more effort, Alessi decided. That was the reason he stood around talking, being polite and accepting congratulations, while others headed off to dance. That was the reason he didn't make his excuses and head home.

Isla watched in mild surprise as her student Flick danced with Tristan, a cardiac surgeon. She could almost feel the sparks coming from them, or was it just that Alessi was standing close?

'Well done,' Isla said, when finally the crowd

gathered around him had dispersed enough for them to have a conversation.

'Thanks,' Alessi said.

'Not too painful?' Isla checked.

'No. Your speech was perfect. I really am very grateful for such a well-run hospital. I just don't like the fact that your father seems to want me to be the poster boy for the NICU.'

'What was that?' Charles came over and Alessi didn't even flinch.

'I was just telling Isla how well run and well equipped the hospital is.'

'Because of nights such as this one,' Charles said. 'You cut it very fine getting here.'

'I already explained that, Dad,' Isla said, but Alessi didn't need Isla to speak for him and told Charles exactly how difficult it had been to get there, albeit a little late.

'I certified a patient dead at eight minutes past six,' Alessi responded coolly, and Isla frowned at the tension between the two men. 'As I said to you at lunch, please don't rely on me to be your front person. I'll do what I can on the social side of things but my job is to keep up the stats while yours is to bring in the funds.'

Isla swallowed. There were few people who spoke to Charles Delamere like that and got away with it, but it was what her father said next that truly confused her.

'You could have at least shaved before you got here.'

'Dad!' Isla was shocked that her father would be so personal but Alessi didn't seem remotely bothered.

'It's fine,' Alessi briefly addressed Isla, then turned his attention back to Charles, who was looking at Alessi with thinly disguised murder in his eyes. 'I stayed with the parents of the baby that died until seven and then I spoke at length with their daughter. Shaving really wasn't my priority.' He looked at Isla. 'Would you like to dance?'

She said yes just to get the two of them apart.

'Alessi, I'm so sorry about that!' Isla said as

they hit the dance floor. She was honestly confused by the way her father was acting. 'I don't know what's wrong with him. He had no right to say anything about you not having shaved.' Privately she was glad that Alessi hadn't shaved—he looked wonderful and she actually ached to feel his jaw against her skin, but she held back from dancing with him the way she wanted to.

'Don't worry about it.' Alessi shrugged.

'Even so, I don't know what's got into him.'

'I do.' Alessi smiled. 'He knows tonight I am going to be sleeping with his daughter.'

'You assume a lot,' Isla croaked as he pulled her in closer.

'I never assume,' Alessi said. 'I just aim high.'

His fingers were stroking her arms and now his cheek was near hers as he spoke, his jaw was all scratchy against her cheek, even more delicious than Isla had predicted, and she found she could barely breathe.

'I thought you were exhausted.'

'Do I feel tired to you?' Alessi said, and Isla guessed he was referring to the hard heat that was nudging at her stomach.

'No.' A single word was all Isla could manage.

'I'm never too tired for you, Isla.'

She was beyond turned on. She wanted to move her face so their mouths could meet, she wanted the wetness of his tongue and the heat of his skin on hers.

Did she tell him how scared she was?

Did she tell him that he would be her first?

Isla would possibly die if he found out she was a virgin.

She'd had an internal when she'd had appendicitis and the doctors had thought it might be an ovarian cyst.

There was going to be no bloodshed, no 'Oh, my God, is that your hymen?' Just utter inexperience in very experienced arms.

Yet she wanted him and she had never till now wanted a man.

She wanted to be made love to and kill this

demon for ever, choke it at the neck and get on with her life.

She knew his reputation, knew his relationships were fleeting at best. This might be just a one-night stand but it would be one that would help her step into her future.

Isla pulled her head back and looked into black, smiling eyes and, no, a heavy heart was not what was needed tonight. A long confessional could not help things here.

It was lust looking back at her, not love, she reminded herself.

Yet it was the beginning of the end of the prison she had trapped herself in and, however unwittingly, Alessi could set her free.

'What are you thinking?' he asked.

'I'm not going to tell you.'

It was the truth and it was also *the* truth.

Isla's decision was made.

Alessi would never know that he was her first.

'I'm going to go soon,' he said in a low voice that made her shiver on the inside. 'I don't want to offend your father by leaving with you. I'll text you my address.'

'You don't know my number.'

'I do,' Alessi said. 'Don't you remember sending me that school reunion photo on the night we met, the night you blew me off?' She was on fire in his arms as he scolded her for her actions that night. 'You're going to apologise *properly* for that tonight.'

'Meaning?'

'Meaning I am going to go and say my goodbyes,' Alessi said. His fingers were at the tie of her halter neck and she had an urge for him to unknot it, to be naked against him, to give in to the kiss that they both craved.

As the song ended, so, too, did their dance and Alessi gave her a brief smile of thanks before walking off.

To the world it might have looked like a duty dance, but for Isla it had been pure pleasure. She joined her father and tried to carry on a conversation with a prominent couple as her heart hammered and her mind whirred as to what to do. She saw Flick leaving with Tristan but this time Isla could only smile with the realisation that she had reprimanded Alessi just a few weeks ago for the very same thing—a doctor seeing one of her students.

She had been jealous, Isla could see it so clearly now.

Her phone buzzed and she glanced at it.

There was no message from Alessi, just his address.

'Heading off already?' Charles frowned. 'It's a bit soon.'

Isla looked at her father. She always did the right thing by her parents, by her sister, by Rupert, by her staff, her patients, by everyone but herself.

It was far from too soon.

Putting herself first was way overdue, in fact.

Isla left without another word.

CHAPTER NINE

ALESSI STEPPED INTO his apartment and swapped the crystal of his award for the crystal of a brandy glass.

He sent a text and wondered.

Would she come?

And if she did, then what would tomorrow bring?

He had spent close to a year wondering about Isla. Disliking her, yet wanting her. A whole year of trying to fathom what went on behind that cool facade.

No one had ever got into his head-space more and yet, rarely for Alessi, he did wonder about the consequences of tonight. He didn't want to be shut down by Isla again, yet a part of him knew it was inevitable. Rare were the glimpses of the true Isla and he found himself craving them. From the first unguarded night to the smile when she had walked out from speaking with Blake and Christine, or sitting on a birthing ball with her teenage mums-to-be.

It was a case of one step forward and a hundred steps back with Isla and, despite the promise of their dance, despite the passion he had felt, Alessi actually doubted now that she'd even turn up at his door.

He checked his phone and, no, she hadn't responded and Alessi found himself scrolling back and looking at their brief communication.

There was an eighteen-year-old Isla, as blonde and as glossy as she was now and smiling for the camera, but there was still that keep-out sign in her eyes. Alessi stared at the image for a long time, zooming in to avoid seeing Talia, for she had no place here tonight. Instead, he looked into Isla's cool gaze and wondered about the secrets she kept, especially when he heard a knock at the door.

'I was wrong,' Alessi said as he opened the door to her. 'I was starting to think you wouldn't come.'

'Why would you think that?' Her voice lied—it was clear, it was confident, it was from the actress she had learnt to be.

'Because you're impossible to read.'

'Better than boring,' she said as he poured her a drink and handed it to her. She didn't like brandy but it was a necessary medicine tonight. She was on the edge of both terror and elation and she wanted her demons gone.

To him.

He really was impossibly beautiful. His tie and jacket were off. If she ignored their surroundings, if she could pretend that they weren't in his apartment, it could almost be the night they'd met for he had been wearing black pants and a white shirt then. He was just as toned, just as sensual, just as confident as he had been that night as he walked over to her, removed her now empty glass from her hand and placed it on a small table. His hands returned to her hips as they had that night, only his mouth did not take hers.

'So...' Alessi looked at her. 'Here we are again.'

He was going to keep to his word, Isla realised as his lips did nothing to meet hers.

'Up to you, Isla.'

Her lips actually ached from his ignoring them, and her body wanted to twitch from the lack of attention she craved. His hands were warm on her hips, his fingers just at the curve of her buttocks, and he moved not a muscle yet he stirred her deep on the inside. 'I thought you were the great seducer,' Isla said, willing her voice to be even, begging her heart to slow down.

'So it's my job to turn you on?' Alessi checked, staring into her eyes.

'Yes.'

'But I already have.'

Was it that simple? Isla thought. Because, yes, he already had.

'You will make the move, Isla.'

Was she here to be served her just deserts, was payback on his mind? She voiced just one of her many fears about this night. 'So you can blow me off this time?'

'God, no.' The need in his voice put paid to that fear and so did his words. 'I wanted you then and I want you now.'

Her eyes told Alessi she wanted him, too. 'So what do you have to say about that night?'

'I'm not going to apologise.'

He shrugged his shoulders but he didn't move and she thought she might die if their lips didn't meet, so she offered her haughty best.

'Sorry!'

'That's a poor excuse for an apology,' Alessi said. 'Say it with your mouth on mine.'

'Alessi…' Isla cringed. She had no idea what was happening, no idea what his game was. She wanted to put up her hand and take a time-out, to consult the rule book, phone a friend, but there was only one other player in this game and she could hardly consult him.

I've never done this before, Alessi, she wanted to reveal. *Apart from one kiss with you, I've never really been intimate or affectionate with a man before...*

Only that wasn't true.

Thirty seconds ago she had never been this intimate or affectionate but now she was pressing her lips to his mouth as if it was the most natural thing in the world. 'Sorry,' Isla breathed, feeling his lips stretch into a smile beneath hers as she joined in the game.

And she'd just been intimate again because her hands were running over his back as she whispered to his lips again.

'I can't hear you,' Alessi said, and her lips moved to his ear, to the lovely, soft lobe, such a contrast to the scratch of his jaw, and she was saying the same word again.

'Sorry.'

Sorry for being a bitch, sorry for shutting you

out, sorry for a year of deprivation when it was so easy after all.

She was unbuttoning his shirt as her mouth moved to his neck. It really was that simple. He shrugged out of his shirt and she ran her hands over the lean chest, stroking his hardening nipples, and all she had to be, Isla realised, was herself, and she knew what she wanted.

It was Isla's fingers rather than Alessi's that undid the halter neck to her dress and the feel of skin, of his firm chest against her naked one, matched the moan that escaped from him, and then she removed her mouth from his neck and stood, taking in the feast going on in his eyes as he looked at her bare breasts.

'I've run out of sorries,' Isla said.

'I haven't.' Alessi's eyes lifted to hers. 'I'm sorry for every terrible thought I have had about you and I'm even sorry for the inappropriate ones—they didn't do you justice…'

His mouth came down on hers then, so hard that Isla thought she might taste blood. Almost a year of anger and pent-up frustration was unleashed from Alessi and for Isla it was electrifying and completely consuming to be so thoroughly kissed. His fierce tongue claimed her as her breasts were crushed to his chest. One of Alessi's hands was at the back of her head, the other on her bottom, yet it was Isla who was pushing in.

She resented the bottom half of her dress for coming between them. She loathed both his trousers and his belt. She wanted them gone, she wanted them both naked, she wanted her legs wrapped around him.

Alessi pulled back and her mouth chased him for more.

'Get on the bed,' he ordered, his words harsh but necessary or they'd be doing it up the wall.

'Where is it?'

He was as disorientated as she and it took a second for him to fathom the familiar route and it was hard getting there while being down each other's throats on the way.

They stripped at the bedroom door, with the

same glee and abandon as if they were taking their clothes off to jump in a river on a hot summer's day. Isla's nerves left her at the door and they dived onto his bed together, want tumbling them over and over, only tearing their mouths from each other to drink in glimpses of the other's nakedness. He loved her large pink areolas and the blonde curls between her legs, and she in turn loved the darkness of his erection that nudged for attention even as his fingers slid inside her.

Isla simply forgot her own inexperience, forgot that she didn't know what to do, or shouldn't know what to do, for all that she *could* do was try and remember to breathe as his fingers deeply stroked her and his mouth noisily worked her breasts.

He touched her where, and in a way, she had never touched herself, and her body flared at the delicious invasion. Her spine seemed to turn to lava and she rocked to his hand.

'Come,' he ordered, and yet she had never done

so. 'Come,' he said urgently, 'because then I'm going to take you...'

She looked down at his fingers sliding in and out of her yet she couldn't relax to his hand, no matter how she wanted to. 'Take me now...'

They were side on and facing each other, and Alessi required no second invitation. His leg nudged hers apart so they scissored his and his fingers moved from deep within and held his thick base and teased, stroking her clitoris, toying at her entrance, till her own hand was closed over his and urged him inside.

'Condom...' He went to reach for one, but that meant rolling, that meant leaving, and her hand stayed steady over his, for she could not bear to break the spell. He nudged in just a little way and her throat closed on itself as she glimpsed how much this was going to hurt. Pain was confirmed again with the second, deeper thrust.

Alessi felt her tension and misread it. Common sense paid a very brief visit and he reached for a condom. The pause as he slid it on was enough for Isla to catch her breath. She didn't like the pale pink of the sheath, she wanted the lovely darkness of before, the softness of his wet skin and the hard feel of him inside. It was that simple, but as he squeezed into her those wants were pale compared to the pleasurable hurt of being taken.

Alessi closed his eyes in pleasure at how tight she was, her moan, her sob, the bite of Isla's teeth on his shoulder spoke not of pain to him.

Or to her.

Yes, it hurt, yes, she wanted a second to regroup, but the salt of his skin in her mouth and the immeasurable force of him thrusting within was a small price to pay for no rest. There were no thoughts to be gathered; he was driving her towards something and Isla was the most willing passenger. She could feel her first orgasm building, each deep stroke of him taking her to the edge of what was surely inevitable, but then Alessi stilled.

'Don't stop,' Isla begged, but then she looked to the reason he had. The condom was shredded, rolled around his base, and decadent wishes came true, because she had loathed him pink and sheathed. She was absolutely on the edge of coming and the sight of him dark inside her simply topped her and it was Isla who took over, who continued the dance, and how could he not join her?

Both were watching, both dizzy with pleasure as Isla came. The first jolt of her body had Isla fight it, scared to let go, but trusting in him she did and with a small scream went with the pleasure. Alessi felt the pulses, the grip of Isla's tight space dragging him in, and he simply gave in and thrust into her, loving the sense of her unleashed. He felt a pull in his stomach and the rise of his balls and somehow, *somehow* there was that brief flash of common sense and he dragged his thick length from her, and both watched as he shot silver over her.

It was delicious to look down while too scary to look up and meet the other's eye.

It had been better than good.

CHAPTER TEN

ISLA WOKE TO the roaming of his hands.

There was a moment of bliss as instinct told her to roll towards him or just lie there and relish the slow exploration, to kiss him as she wanted to, and then she remembered the sheer recklessness of last night.

It was Alessi who addressed it.

'You owe Blake and Christine an apology,' Alessi said to her ear as he kissed it. 'It *is* possible to get too carried away.'

'It's fine,' Isla said, and somehow her voice sounded together. 'I've got it covered.'

He would assume, of course, that this good-time girl would have contraception all taken care of, especially as she was a midwife.

Isla closed her eyes on sudden tears.

What the hell would he say if he knew she'd been a virgin until last night, that she wasn't even on the Pill?

Isla was starting to panic, not that she would let him see.

'I have to go.' She rolled over and gave him a smile.

'Now?'

'Now.' Isla nodded.

'Hey…' His hand was on her shoulder as she sat up. 'There's no need to rush off.'

But there was.

She had to get home.

She had to think.

And so she climbed from the bed and headed out to the lounge, where her clothes lay strewn.

'I'll drive you,' Alessi said as she pulled on her dress.

The embarrassment of getting a taxi in last night's clothes was the only reason she agreed.

Alessi made do with last night's clothes also and the lack of conversation in the car had him rolling his eyes. 'I knew that you'd do this,' he said as he pulled up at a café.

'Do what?'

Alessi gave a mirthless laugh and got out and Isla sat there, watching him order coffee through the café window. Next door the shutters were going up on a pharmacy. Once home she could go and get the morning-after pill, Isla thought, and then closed her eyes because she knew that she wouldn't. She had nothing against others taking it, it just wasn't for her.

She sat there, telling herself she was overreacting, that she couldn't be pregnant, except her assurances had the same ring to her as her teenage mums' did.

She was twenty-eight!

Damn you, Alessi, Isla thought as he walked back to the car carrying coffee. *Damn you for making me lose my head.*

Not just last night but this morning, too, for she wanted more of him. She wanted that grim mouth to smile, she wanted his kiss and to be back in his bed, she wanted more of whatever it was they'd found.

'Here.' He handed her a coffee and Isla took a sip and screwed up her face.

'I don't take sugar.'

'How the hell would I know?' Alessi said as he started the engine. 'Because you don't communicate...'

Her shoulders moved as she let out a small involuntary laugh. 'Did you plan that?'

'I did.' He glanced over and gave her a smile. 'I actually know that you don't take sugar so I asked them to put in three.

'What's your address?' he asked, and after she had given it to him he resumed the conversation. 'Do you know how I know that you don't take sugar?'

Isla said nothing, just stared ahead as he answered his own question.

'Because I don't really like how I am around you, Isla. I don't like it that even though you run so very cold, I still find myself hanging out for the occasional heat. I notice things about you that I would prefer not to. Like you don't have sugar, like the day you told someone you were going to walk in your lunch break yet you never have. How you hold back on everyone and everything…'

'I don't.'

'You do.' Alessi glanced over as he drove her home. She was back to being unreadable, back to being cool and aloof and just everything that she hadn't been last night, and he wanted her back.

'We're going out this afternoon,' he said as they pulled up at her apartment.

'I've got plans.'

'Cancel them. I'll pick you up at one.'

'I might be out.'

'Then I'll be back at two.'

'Alessi…' Isla didn't know what to make of this. 'Last night—'

'I don't want to hear you regret it,' Alessi interrupted, 'or that it was something that shouldn't have happened or that it was just a one-off. Get it into your head that I'm going to date you, Isla, and that starts today. I'm certainly not waiting until Monday to find out if you're speaking to me or avoiding me.'

Isla let out a pale smile. 'It would have been the latter.'

'Which is why we are going out today. There is one thing we need to get straight though, Isla—I don't cheat, and I expect the same from you.' Her cheeks were on fire as he continued speaking. She knew he was referring to the night when she had practically offered to get off with him while Rupert and Amber had been back in the bar. 'I don't care what you got up to when you were with Rupert but if you are seeing me, then you are seeing only me. Do you get that?'

Isla nodded but her heart was heavy.

He really didn't know her at all.

'We have a companion,' Alessi said, when Isla opened her door at one to find him there, holding Niko in his arms. 'Allegra's husband, Steve, is working and she called and asked if I would mind having Niko for the afternoon as she needs a break. She rarely asks…'

'That's fine.' Isla smiled. 'Hi, there, Niko.'

'I thought we could go to the zoo,' Alessi said, but he must have seen her startle. 'You don't like the zoo?'

'I've never been,' Isla admitted. 'Actually, that's not strictly true, I've been to a couple of dinners there and a wedding once. I've just never…'

'*Been* to the zoo,' Alessi finished for her. 'Well, I have been many times. It's Niko's favorite place for me to take him.'

'I'd better get changed,' Isla said, because she'd put on a dress, assuming they would be going out for lunch. 'Jeans?'

'Shorts,' Alessi said. 'It will get hot walking around and, anyway, I like to see your legs.'

How could he manage to flirt while holding a three-year-old as well as offering to take her to the zoo, of all places?

* * *

It was hot and smelly and actually fun.

'Oh, my…' Isla fell in love with the orang-utans, which was possibly to be expected, given her job, but the babies were so adorable.

'They are as hairy as some of my premmies,' Alessi said.

Isla glanced at him, hearing the genuine warmth in his voice.

'*Your* premmies?'

'Until they go home.' Alessi nodded.

'Wouldn't that take its toll?'

'Perhaps, but the night that my brother died it looked as if my parents might lose all three of us. There was a doctor there who stayed night after night and my parents always say that were it not for him, they could have gone home with no children.'

'That's your parents' memory, Alessi,' Isla said, ignoring the set of his jaw. It worried her, all the pressure that he put on himself. 'I'm sure there were a whole lot of others who played their part.'

'I don't need to be told to delegate.'

'Lucky you, then,' Isla said, ignoring the edge to Alessi's voice that told her this was out of bounds. 'I'm constantly being reminded to delegate by my team. Anyway, I just hope your phone's off, because I've never been to the zoo before and I might prove a terrible disappointment for Niko if you suddenly have to dash off.'

He gave a reluctant smile, which turned to a wry one an hour or so later when Jed rang through some results that Alessi was waiting for.

'Thanks for letting me know,' Alessi said. 'Yes, just continue with the regime.' As he ended the call Alessi looked over at Isla. 'I'll never turn my phone off.'

Isla just laughed. 'Neither will I.'

They just wandered, eating ice cream and taking it in turns to push Niko in his stroller. 'He gets tired,' Alessi explained. 'He's walking so much better now but on days like today it's better to bring the stroller along.'

'How bad was he when he was born?' Isla asked.

'Bad enough that we thought he might not make it,' he said. 'Allegra was very sick, too. It was a terrible time. My parents...' He was quiet for a moment. 'I think it brought a lot back for them.'

'About your brother?'

Alessi nodded but then tried to turn the conversation a little lighter. 'God, could you imagine the pressure if anything had happened to Allegra?'

'Pressure?'

'"Do your homework, Alessi, your brother would have loved the chance. When are you going to get married...?"' He rolled his eyes. '"Your brother would have loved that chance, too!"' He gave a wry smile. 'Thankfully Allegra and Steve have taken some of that heat off by marrying and having Niko. Don't get me wrong, I love my parents but they make it clear that I'm not doing all the things a good Greek son should.'

'Well, I don't do all the things that a good Delamere girl should.'

'Such as?' Alessi asked as they headed towards the elephants and he took Niko out of the stroller and put him onto his shoulders.

'Such as being a midwife. My parents thought I should study medicine, like my sister. It caused a lot of rows. Even when I got the position of head midwife my father suggested I'd be better off heading to medical school. Finally, though, he seems to get that it's not a hobby.'

'Don't you get on with them?'

'Oh, I do,' Isla said. 'We've had our differences. My midwifery for one, and that they were pretty absent when we were growing up. I get on much better with them now that I'm an adult. I can understand better why, now—their charity work is really important.'

'Family is more so.'

'I agree,' Isla said. 'I guess it's all about balance. My parents didn't have that, it was all or nothing for them.'

They stopped at the elephants. A calf had recently been born and there was quite a crowd gathered. 'Imagine delivering that,' Isla grinned.

'You love your job, don't you?' Alessi said, feeling more than a touch guilty at his assumption that her father had paved her way—clearly she'd had to fight to get where she was.

'I do.'

'Did you always want to be a midwife?'

'Not always,' Isla said, but didn't elaborate. She just watched as the little calf peeked out from between his mother's legs.

'I love the elephants,' Alessi said into the silence. 'I like the way they always remember.'

'I hate the way they always remember,' Isla said.

'Why?'

'Because some things are best forgotten.'

'Such as?' Alessi asked.

She turned and gave a weak smile but shook

her head. She simply didn't know how to tell him or how to answer his questions about when she had decided to be a midwife. At what point did you hand over your heart, your past? At what point did you reveal others' secrets?

Isla didn't know.

'He's getting tired,' Alessi said as he lowered Niko from his shoulders. 'We'll take him to see his favourite thing and then get him home.'

'What is Niko's favourite thing?' Isla asked, glad for the change in subject.

It was the meerkats!

Niko hung over the edge of the barrier, shrieking with laughter every time they stood up and froze, calling out to ''Lessi' to watch.

'Look at that one,' Alessi said to Niko. 'He's on lookout while the others dig for food.'

Niko didn't care if he was on lookout; he just laughed and laughed till in the end so, too, were Isla and Alessi.

It was fun.

Just a fun day out and Isla hadn't had too

many of those. She finally felt as if she was being herself, only it was a new self, someone she had never been—someone who was honest and open, except for the lies she had promised to keep.

At six, Alessi strapped an already fast asleep Niko into his car seat. 'Hopefully he will stay that way till tomorrow,' he said. 'I'll get him home and then we can go and get some dinner.'

'Won't it look odd if I'm with you?' Isla asked.

'Odd?' Alessi checked.

'For Allegra, seeing me out with you…'

'I'm not going to hide you around the corner and pretend that I've spent the day with Niko alone. Anyway, he's three, he's going to tell her that you were there.'

'I guess.' There was a flutter in her stomach as they pulled up at Allegra's house, but thankfully Alessi didn't put her through the torture of coming up to the door when Isla said that she'd prefer to wait for him in the car.

'I'll just carry him up the stairs and put him into bed,' Alessi said. 'I won't be long.'

Famous last words.

'Is that Isla in the car?' Allegra asked as she let him in.

'It is.'

'Alessi…' Allegra started, but didn't elaborate until Niko was tucked up in bed and the bedroom door was closed behind him.

'What?' Alessi said. He'd heard the note of reprimand in his sister's voice when she'd seen who was in the car. 'It's no big deal.'

'Well, it is to me,' Allegra said. 'Can you try and not break up with *this one* before I have the baby. I don't want any bad feelings…'

'There won't be any bad feelings,' Alessi said. 'Isla would never involve you like that…' Then he halted, because he'd lied. It *was* starting to feel like a big deal. 'Anyway, I have no intention of breaking things up.'

Allegra gave a slightly disbelieving snort. 'The baby's still four weeks off, Alessi.'

'I know.'

Allegra paused at the bottom of the stairs and turned and looked at her brother, who she loved very much. 'Four weeks would be an all-time record,' Allegra said. 'Well, not an all-time...' Her voice trailed off. She didn't think the mention of Talia's name would be particularly welcome here. 'I like Isla.'

'I do, too.' Alessi admitted. 'Yes, perhaps it would be more sensible to wait till the baby is born but...' He gave a small shrug. 'I'd already waited for nearly a year.'

He had.

Alessi said goodbye to his sister and then headed back to the car. A part of him wanted to turn and retract what he'd said to his sister—push the genie back in the bottle—yet he did really like Isla.

He more than liked her, in fact.

It was a rather new feeling to have.

'Right.' Alessi climbed into the driver's seat. 'Do you want to go for dinner?'

'I do.' Isla smiled. 'I'm actually starving.'

'Name where you want to go, then,' Alessi said. 'I picked the zoo so it's your turn to choose.'

Isla thought for a moment. 'We could go to Geo's. I hear they've got a new menu.'

'Geo's?' Alessi frowned but then screwed up his nose. 'Maybe we could try somewhere else...'

'Why?' Isla pushed. 'You're Greek and I love Greek food and they do the best in Melbourne.'

'We'll never get a booking this time on a Sunday night.'

'I will,' Isla said.

'They have a dress code,' Alessi pointed out.

'Not for me...' She halted then. Geo's was one of the best Greek restaurants in Melbourne and it was booked out ages in advance, just not for the likes of Isla. She could feel the tension in the car and guessed it was thanks to her latest arrogant remark. God, she'd suggested a seriously expensive restaurant in the same way she'd asked for champagne the first night they'd met.

'Don't make me feel pretentious, Alessi.'

'I'm not.'

'Actually, you are.'

He could have driven off, Alessi realised, simply left it at that. Instead, he left the engine idling and told her the truth. 'Geo's is actually my parents' restaurant, Isla.' He watched as her eyes widened in surprise and then he surprised himself and let out the handbrake. 'Let's go there.'

'Alessi.' Isla let out a nervous laugh. 'I honestly didn't know. I don't want to make things awkward for you.'

'Why would be it awkward?' he said, while determined not to make it so.

The restaurant was packed and heads turned as Alessi led her through. Isla was acutely aware that she was wearing shorts and runners, especially when a woman, who had to be his mother, came over and gave her son a kiss.

'This is Isla,' Alessi introduced them. 'She's a friend from work and we have just taken Niko to the zoo. Isla, this is my mother, Yolanda.'

'Come upstairs,' Yolanda said. 'Introduce Isla...'

'We're going to eat downstairs,' Alessi said

firmly, and guided Isla to a table near the back. And as they took a seat he explained. 'If I take you upstairs then I'd have to marry you,' he teased.

'Downstairs it is, then.'

The food was amazing—even if Yolanda did tend to hover. Isla could hear laughter from upstairs. It was clear that Alessi had a huge extended family and a couple of them stopped by, greeting Isla warmly.

'Your family are close,' Isla said.

'Very,' Alessi agreed, and then told her a little about how the restaurant had started. 'We started getting more and more orders for catering. People would bring in their own dishes and ask my mother to make her moussaka in them so that they could pass them off as their own. Once we had finished school my parents were ready to take the gamble so the café was closed and Geo's opened. Upstairs is all for family. Downstairs is the main restaurant.'

'Do you come here a lot?'

'I try to drop in once a week,' Alessi said,

'maybe once a fortnight if things are busy at work.'

'And have you ever taken anyone upstairs?' Isla smiled, more than a little nosy where Alessi was concerned.

'One person.'

The smile was wiped from her face as she heard the serious note in his voice. 'You remember Talia from school?'

Isla nodded.

'We started going out when she first went to med school.'

'How long were you going out for?' Isla asked, and his response caught her by surprise.

'Two years.'

'Oh.' She'd always thought Alessi kept his relationships short-term. 'That's a long time.'

'Especially by Greek standards,' Alessi said, and took a breath. He never went into the past with women but he was starting to hope for more of a future with Isla, and for Alessi that meant being honest. 'We were about to get engaged.

Neither my parents nor hers have ever forgiven me for calling it off.'

'You were young.' Isla tried to keep things light. 'Surely that's better if you weren't sure you were ready.'

'I was ready,' Alessi said, and watched as Isla's glass paused just a little before she placed it on the table. He was close to sharing, closer than he had ever been. He liked her take on things, he actually respected her directness and the slight detachment that came from Isla. She offered a rare perspective and he wanted more of that now. 'Apart from the reunion, do you keep in touch with Talia?' Alessi asked.

'A bit,' she said. 'Just social networks and things… Why?' She smiled. 'Do you still have a thing for her?'

'God, no,' Alessi said. It was the truth.

He looked at Isla—the fact that she and Talia were loosely in touch was enough of a reason not to tell her the truth about that time.

Or an *excuse* not to.

Isla would never break a confidence, he knew that.

Alessi knew then how serious he was about Isla because in more than a decade he had never once come close to telling another woman the truth behind that time.

But not here.

Not yet.

'How serious did you and Rupert get?' Alessi asked. 'Did you ever speak of marriage?'

'No.' Isla let out a short laugh. 'Rupert and I…'

Alessi watched as she suddenly took great interest in the dessert menu, which two minutes ago Isla had declined, and he was suddenly glad he hadn't revealed all.

Yes, he knew her a bit better but despite her apparent ease, Isla still revealed very little. 'Shall we go?' Alessi suggested, and Isla nodded.

'It seems strange not to have to wait for the bill.'

'We still have to account for our time.' Alessi smiled and rolled his eyes as his mother made her way over, insisting that they come upstairs for coffee, but Alessi declined.

'I have work at seven,' he said, determined not to let his family push things, while determined not to hide. 'So does Isla.'

He drove her back to her apartment and they chatted along the way. 'Do you miss Isabel?' Alessi asked.

'I do,' Isla said, 'though it sounds as if she's having an amazing time in Cambridge...'

'How come she went?' Alessi asked. 'It was quite sudden.'

'It just came up,' Isla said, and gave him the same answer that she had to Sean. 'Who wouldn't kill for twelve months' secondment in England?'

'It had nothing to do with Sean?'

'Sean?'

'I just picked up on something.' Alessi glanced over. 'When he first started, I was down on MMU and Isabel was blushing and avoiding him as much as you would have avoided me tomorrow had I not dragged you out today...'

'I don't know what you're talking about.'

She did, Alessi was sure, but her trust was worth his patience and so he kissed her instead.

His kiss was more intimate than last night, Isla thought. It tasted not so much of passion but of promise and possibility. His mouth was more familiar and yet more intriguing because it pushed her further along a path she had never been on with a man.

Here they could end their amazing weekend.

Right now she could climb out of the car and go up to her apartment. Both of them could gather their thoughts, ready to resume normal service on Monday.

It was Isla who pulled back. 'I don't want anyone at work to know…'

'Of course,' Alessi said, and then guessed the reason they were still in his car, rather than her asking him up. 'Oh, yes, you share with Darcie.' He hesitated, wondering if asking her back to his for a second night was too much, too soon, yet it was Isla's boldness that took him by delighted surprise.

'She's on call tonight.'

It was new, it was delicious, it was a weekend that didn't have to end just yet as Isla invited him just a little bit further into her life.

CHAPTER ELEVEN

FOR A WOMAN who had never dated, Isla got a crash course and the next two weeks were blissful. Even the hard parts, like attending Archie's funeral in the hospital chapel, were made better for being together.

'Thanks for everything you did, Isla,' Donna said as they said their farewells after the service. 'Especially with Jessica.'

'How is she doing?' Isla asked.

'She's upset, of course, but she really does know that none of this was her fault. She's so glad that they had that lovely evening together and that last day.' Donna turned to Alessi. 'Thank…' she attempted, then broke down, and Alessi gave her a cuddle.

'He was such a beautiful boy,' he said. 'I am

so sorry that there wasn't more that could be done. You made the right choice, Donna. He got a whole day of being loved and cuddled by his mum and dad and big sister.'

Isla, who never cried, could feel tears at the backs of her eyes as Donna wept and nodded and then pulled away. 'I need to get back up to the unit for Elijah.'

'Go,' Alessi said. 'I will see you up there soon.'

He walked up towards Maternity with Isla. He'd felt her standing rigid beside him during the service and had noted that not a tear had been shed by her.

'Awful, wasn't it?' Alessi said.

'Yep.'

'Does nothing move you to tears, Isla?'

She halted and turned to face him. 'Excuse me?'

'I'm just commenting…'

'What, because I don't break down and cry I'm not upset?'

'I never said that,' Alessi answered calmly. 'I

was just asking if anything moves you to tears. Babies' funerals are very difficult.'

'I agree.'

'Why do you hold back?'

'What, because I don't cry…'

'You hold back in everything, Isla,' he said.

It wasn't a row, more an observation, and one Isla pondered as she set up that night for TMTB.

She was pleased to see that Ruby was back.

'Are we getting pizza tonight?' Ruby asked, and Isla nodded.

'We are. I've already ordered it so it should be here soon. How are you doing, Ruby?'

'I've got my scan tomorrow afternoon.'

'Is anyone coming with you?' Isla asked, and Ruby shook her head. 'Would you like me to come with you?'

'No, thanks.'

'Well, if you change your mind just ask them to page me.'

As everyone gathered there was one noticeable absence and Isla was delighted to tell the group the happy news. 'Alison had a little girl on Monday,' Isla said. 'The birth went really well and the baby is beautiful. I've got a photo on my phone that Alison asked me to show you.'

Her phone was passed around and Isla loved watching the smile on each of the young women's faces. It was always a nice time but it was also a little confronting for some of the group as they realised that some day soon it would be their baby being spoken about in the group. Clearly it was too much for Ruby because she quickly passed on the phone.

Isla was worried for the young girl and though Ruby hung around afterwards to take the last of the pizza, still she didn't want to speak with Isla and made her excuses and dashed off.

She needed someone she gelled with, Isla thought. Isla took no offence that that person might not be herself and the next day, when Ruby didn't page Isla to come for the ultrasound, Isla was actually trying to think who might be the best fit for Ruby when her pager went off.

'Isla, it's Darcie. I was wondering if you could come down to the antenatal clinic. I've got a patient, Ruby, and—'

'I know Ruby.' Isla smiled. 'Did she change her mind?'

'Sorry?'

'I offered to come with her for her ultrasound but she said no.'

'Well, she's asked for you now. Isla, there's an anomaly on the ultrasound. The baby has spina bifida. The poor kid has had the most terrible afternoon. Loads of tests and specialists. Heinz was speaking with her and she's got terribly upset...'

Isla groaned. As brilliant as Heinz, a paediatric neurologist, was, his people skills weren't the best. 'He broached termination and Ruby is beside herself.'

'I'll be there now. Who's the midwife?' Isla asked, wondering why she hadn't been told about this long ago. She knew Ruby's ultrasound had been scheduled for two.

'Lucas,' Darcie said, and then hesitated. 'I didn't call him in till just before that.'

'I don't know what's going on between the two of you,' Isla said swiftly, 'but sort it out. I don't care if you don't get on, I don't care if you're my flatmate. I care about my patients.'

She was furious as she walked down the corridor but took a calming breath as she stepped into the room. Lucas was sitting with a teary Ruby, who had clearly been through the wringer. She looked so young and vulnerable and she should have had an advocate with her, a friend, anyone, but instead she'd faced it all pretty much alone.

'It's okay, Ruby…' Isla said, but it was the wrong thing to say because an angry Ruby jumped to her feet.

'No, it isn't!' Ruby said. 'I've just been told that it isn't all right…'

'Ruby,' Isla said, 'I know it's so much to take in.' She just wanted to get her away from the clinic for a while, to talk to her without everyone hanging around. 'Why don't we go to the canteen?'

'I don't want to go the canteen with you, you stuck-up cow,' Ruby said. 'I just want…' She didn't finish but instead ran off. Isla went after her but she knew it was pointless.

'She just needs some time,' Darcie said when Isla saw her.

'I know,' Isla said, and looked at Darcie. 'I should have been told. Just because you and Lucas aren't talking—'

'Hey!' Darcie broke in. 'Lucas did a CTG on a thirty-five-weeker at two and found no heart-beat. I'm going to deliver her tonight. He's been brilliant, he's been in with Mum and Dad all afternoon. Yes, we've had a row and we don't get on, but my not telling him about Ruby had nothing to do with that. We were swamped. I had no idea Heinz was going to talk to her, I just thought he was looking through the scans.'

'Isla—'

Isla turned as Lucas knocked on the door. 'Allegra Manos is here, she said you were to be paged when she arrived.'

'Thanks.'

'I'm sorry I didn't let you know about Ruby,' Lucas added. 'I was in with a mum—'

'Darcie explained.' Isla let out a tense breath. 'Sorry about that, Darcie.'

'Apology accepted.' Darcie smiled. 'It's just been one of those awful afternoons.'

Not that the other patients could know that, so both Isla and Darcie pushed out a smile and went in to see Allegra.

She looked fantastic and the baby seemed to be doing just fine.

'Everything,' Darcie said as she examined Allegra, 'is looking great. The baby is head down and a nice size and there's lots of fluid. How are the movements?'

'Lots of them,' Allegra said.

Darcie spoke at length with Allegra about a trial of labour and told her that they would part insert an epidural. 'It won't stop you from moving around but it means that if we do need to move to a Caesarean then everything will be set up, so we can move quickly if we have to and you can also stay awake.'

Darcie answered a few more of Allegra's questions. 'I'll be seeing you weekly from now on,' Darcie said as she stepped out.

'All looks good.' Isla smiled.

'Can you let Alessi know that for me? I know he'll be itching to find out. He's doing his best not to ring for updates.'

'I'll let him know,' Isla said, but when she paged him she got the head nurse in Neonatology, who said he was busy with an infant. 'Can I pass on a message?'

'It's fine,' Isla said. 'I'll try again later.'

Much later.

In fact, it was after eight when she made her way up to NICU and buzzed and was let in, and after washing her hands she was directed to Alessi, who was by little Elijah's cot. 'How is he?' she asked.

'Giving me far too many sleepless nights, but he's doing a bit better,' he said. He was putting an IV in Elijah's scalp and Isla stood quietly as Alessi concentrated. There was a little picture attached to his cot of him and Archie lying together on what must have been Archie's last day, and Isla tore her eyes from it as Alessi finished and peeled off his gloves. 'Thank you,' he said to the neonatal nurse who had assisted him. 'Is this a personal visit?' he asked as they walked from the cot.

'Sort of.' Isla nodded. 'I'm just here to tell you about Allegra. All went well—'

'We'll go into my office.'

Isla followed him in. 'Your office is very messy.'

'Because I'm never in it long enough to put anything away,' he said, and as a case in point his phone buzzed and he answered it. 'I'll be out in a few moments.' He then hung up the phone. 'How is Allegra?'

'Fantastic. It's all progressing well. The baby

is head down and engaged and Darcie will be seeing her weekly from now on.'

'She still wants a trial of labour?'

'She does,' Isla replied. 'Darcie has gone through it all with her and Allegra will have an epidural placed just in case a Caesarean is needed.' She perched on the edge of his desk. 'What time are you finishing?' she asked, knowing that he should already be off now.

'I'm just waiting for some results to come in on Elijah.'

'I thought he was doing a bit better?'

'He is,' he said. 'I just want to check his labs.'

'Who's on call tonight?'

'Jed,' Alessi clipped.

'Can't Jed—'

'Isla, please don't,' Alessi warned, because this really was his tipping point. 'I work long hours. If it doesn't suit—'

'Oh, please.' She simply laughed in the face of his warning. 'I'm not some needy miss, worried that you're going to ruin dinner if you're late home.' She pulled him towards her and started to kiss his tired mouth. 'And I'm not trying to come between you and your premmies.' She locked her hands behind his neck and looked into the blackest, most beautiful eyes she had ever seen and was as honest as she had ever been. 'I don't care if you're here till five in the morning just as long as you need to be here, Alessi…I just happen to care about you. If you were one of my staff I'd have sent you home about three hours ago. In fact, I'd have told you to take tomorrow off, too.'

'I'm not one of your staff.'

'Lucky for you.'

Alessi looked at Isla. He loved how she'd bypassed his warning, how she'd admitted she cared, so he told her the truth.

'I can't send Donna and Tom home with no baby.'

'And you'll do everything to see that you don't,' Isla calmly assured him. 'But Elijah's going to be here for weeks, maybe months…'

She could see the wrestle in his eyes. 'I'm not going to push it.' She gave him another quick kiss and jumped down from the desk. 'I'm heading home. Stop by if it's not too late.'

'Is Darcie on call tonight?'

'Nope.' Isla headed for the door. 'I doubt she'll drop dead with shock—half the hospital seems to have worked out that we're on.'

They *were* on.

Alessi knew that when at ten, instead of crashing in the on-call room, he was driving to Isla's. It had nothing to do with the promise of sex. He would probably be kicked out for snoring, he was so tired. It was balance, it was her, it was the calm of non-judgment and the freedom of choice along with cool reason.

'I'd just about given up,' Isla said, answering the door in her dressing gown, her hair wrapped in a towel.

'Jed might call,' he warned her. 'I might need to go in.'

'That's fine,' she said. 'Do you want something to eat?'

'I had something earlier,' he said. 'I'd kill for a shower, though.'

He'd been to the apartment a few times but never while Darcie was there. She was tapping away on her computer while watching a movie and didn't seem remotely fazed to see him here.

'Help yourself,' Isla said, opening her bedroom door.

Alessi did.

To shampoo, to conditioner, to Isla's deodorant.

'You smell like me,' Isla said as he joined her in bed and then kissed him. 'You taste like me, too.'

Alessi really hadn't come here with sex on his mind and that became more apparent as their kiss deepened. 'I didn't bring anything…'

'Alessi.'

'Can we lose the condoms?' he asked. 'I don't care what tests, I'll do them, but…'

They were just so completely into each other that this conversation had only been a matter of time but Isla was grateful for the very small reprieve he had just given her.

'Yes…' She knew she should tell him there was no need for tests on her part and she would, Isla decided. She was moving closer and closer to opening up to him, just not now. Now she could feel his exhaustion, now it was so easy to be bold, to just move her lips from his mouth and kiss downwards, to hold him in her hands and feel him grow.

For Alessi it was heaven.

Her tentative lips did not alert him to her inexperience. Instead he just revelled in her slow explorations and the trail of her damp hair down his body.

Isla tasted him for the first time, loved the feel of his hand on her head and the gentle pressure that pushed her deeper. Selfish was his pleasure and that she revelled in. She could feel his occasional restraint, when he tried not to thrust.

Then there was the turn-on when he stopped trying and just gave in. The power, the feel, the taste, the rush of him coming had Isla come, too, at the intimate private pleasure, and then afterwards, feeling him relaxed and sated beside her, it was the closest she had ever felt to another person.

And Alessi felt it, too, for there in the dark, as pleasure receded, a deeper connection flowed in as she lay in his arms.

'I was wrong to accuse you of holding back when there are things that I haven't told you.'

Isla looked at him as he continued speaking.

'Talia was pregnant.' It was with Isla that he shared for the first time. 'When she told me I asked her to marry me and we decided to tell our parents about the pregnancy after the wedding.' He liked it that her face was still there, though her smile had gone, and he liked it that she didn't ask questions. 'We had a big dinner at the restaurant on the Saturday…'

He tried to explain better. 'In Greek families

you establish a connection before the man asks the woman's father, so even though we weren't officially engaged, it was a given that it was to come. On the Wednesday Talia missed lectures. I went over to check if all was okay and it was clear she was unwell. I thought she was losing the baby. I wanted her to go to hospital but she told me there was no need…' He watched Isla's slight frown. 'She told me then that she'd had an abortion that morning.'

'Without telling you?'

'Yep. She thought I would try to talk her out of it. She said that she wanted to have children one day but that she knew she couldn't study to be a doctor and be a teenage mum…' Alessi turned from Isla and looked back at the ceiling. 'I get that, I understand that. I get that it was her body…'

'It was your baby, though?'

Alessi nodded and he waited and hoped for Isla to share.

'Go to sleep,' Isla said, and Alessi smiled into the darkness.

If it took for ever he would find out what went on in that head, and then he smiled into the darkness again. 'Jed and I have swapped. I'm working this weekend.'

'But you're already on call twice next week,' Isla pointed out sleepily.

'I know,' Alessi said, 'but it will be worth it to have next weekend off. You know what next weekend is?' he checked. 'Valentine's Day. The anniversary of when we first met.'

'And?'

'I have plans for us.'

'Such as?'

'You'll find out,' he said. Yes, he'd had plans when he'd swapped the work arrangements with Jed—an intimate meal with Isla, perhaps a night in a gorgeous hotel, but right now those plans were getting bigger and he gave a wry laugh.

'Hopefully it will end better than the last one.'

CHAPTER TWELVE

IT WAS THE promise of the weekend and the fact that her period was due that had Isla knocking on Darcie's office door on the Monday morning.

'Hi, Darcie…'

'Hey, Isla.'

'I was wondering…' Isla started, but then she changed her mind. She would make an appointment with her GP, Isla decided, and turned to go. Except her period was due any time and for it to be safe she'd need to start the Pill on her first day. She also knew that she needed to have her blood pressure checked and things… So Isla took a breath. 'Have you got a moment?'

'Sure,' Darcie said. 'I've got precisely six.' She frowned when Isla didn't smile. 'I've got all the time you need, Isla. Is everything okay?'

'Oh, it's not a biggie,' Isla said. 'It won't take long. I was just wondering if you could write me a script for the Pill…'

'Sure,' Darcie said. 'Have a seat.'

Isla did, though again she was tempted to change her mind. 'What do you usually take?' Darcie asked, pulling out a blood-pressure cuff. When Isla didn't immediately answer, Darcie said, 'Sorry, Isla, but I'm not just going to give you a repeat without checking your blood pressure.'

Isla nodded. She knew that Darcie was thorough and was starting to realise what a stupid idea this had been as Darcie quickly checked it. 'All good.' Darcie nodded. 'So, what are you on?'

'I'm not,' Isla said.

'What type of contraception do you usually use?'

'Condoms,' Isla said, and then cleared her throat.

'Okay,' Darcie answered carefully. They both knew that condoms weren't the safest of choices.

'Look, sorry, Darcie, I should have gone to my GP. I just—'

'Isla, it's fine.' Darcie interrupted. 'I'm not just going to write out a script, though, if it's something that you haven't taken before.'

Isla nodded.

'Have you any history that I should know about?'

Isla shook her head.

'Blood clots, migraines…' She went through the list of contraindications.

'Nothing.'

'Good.' Darcie smiled. 'When did you last have a smear test?'

Isla sat there, her cheeks on fire.

'Sorry, I keep forgetting I'm in Australia,' Darcie said into the silence. 'When did you last have a Pap?'

Isla had never had a Pap because she'd never been sexually active.

'It's been…' Isla gave a tight shrug. 'It's been a while.'

'I'm not going to tell you off for leaving it too long,' Darcie said. 'Let's just get it over and done with. When is your period due?'

'Today or tomorrow.'

'Have you had any unprotected sex?'

'No.' Isla shook her head, but more to clear it. What the hell was she lying for? 'Once,' she amended. 'But he… ' She let out a breath in embarrassment. God, no wonder the patients loathed all the questions. 'He withdrew.'

'Did you do it standing up?' Darcie grinned as she teased. They'd both heard it all before and knew that withdrawal was far from safe.

'I'm not pregnant,' Isla said. She knew that she wasn't—her breasts had that heavy feeling they always got when her period was near. Not that it put Darcie off.

'Fine, then you won't mind peeing in a jar to put my mind at ease. Then I'm going to do a Pap and give you a work-up and get all the boxes ticked so you can hopefully forget about things for another couple of years.'

'You don't have time.'

'I just made time.' Darcie smiled. She was a thorough doctor and refused to be rushed by anyone, especially her patients, and a little while later as she looked at the pregnancy card on the desk before her, a patient Isla suddenly was.

'Isla,' Darcie said, and Isla watched as she pushed the card over to her.

Isla stared at it for a long moment. There were possibly a thousand thoughts in her head but not a single one of them did she show on her face. She just looked up at Darcie.

'Can we leave the Pap for another time?' Isla said, her voice completely clear, her expression unreadable.

'Of course, but, Isla—'

'Can we not discuss this, please?' Isla stood. 'Just…' She turned as she got to the door. 'You won't tell anyone…'

'You don't have to ask me that, Isla,' Darcie

said, and Isla nodded. 'But if you want to talk any time, you can.'

Isla muttered brief thanks and headed out to her department, and for the first time ever she left early.

She lay on her bed and just stared at the ceiling and all she felt was stupid, naïve and embarrassed at having got pregnant her *first* time.

It was all she could manage to feel as she lay there.

When the phone bleeped to indicate a text, she knew it was from Alessi but she didn't even look at it.

She simply could not bear to think of telling him or even attempt to fathom his reaction.

Far worse than his anger would be duty.

Isla lay there, recalling his words—how he'd done the right thing by Talia, how he'd offered to marry her as soon as he'd found out.

She didn't want that for either of them.

They'd been going out for a couple of weeks,

which surely meant, given his track record, that they had just about run their course.

Isla tried to comfort herself, reminded herself that the reason she'd been going on the Pill in the first place was that Alessi himself had wanted to move things forward, to lose the condoms.

On the proviso that she was on the Pill, though.

Isla felt a tear slide out and she screwed her eyes shut.

She heard the door open and Darcie come home and Isla wanted to call out to her, she wanted to sob, hell, she wanted to break down and cry.

But she didn't know how to, scared that if she let out a part of her fear then the rest would come gushing out.

Secrets she had sworn never to reveal.

CHAPTER THIRTEEN

ISLA DIDN'T HAVE to try too hard to avoid Alessi.

That night he was too wrecked to even drive home so he sent a text to Isla to say he was crashing at the hospital. About two seconds after hitting 'send' he did just that in the on-call room on the unit.

He dived back into work at eight the next day when he was on call again. He finally saw Isla on Tuesday but it wasn't a social visit—a newborn was rapidly deteriorating and all Alessi wanted from Isla was her cool efficiency, which he got.

In fact, Isla was doing her very best to keep calm.

Wrestling with her own news, trying to fathom that she herself would, in a matter of months, be a mum, she had been checking on a newborn when she found a baby looking dusky at her mother's breast. Isla moved the infant, hoping her breathing had just been obstructed temporarily but was silently alarmed by her colour and tone.

'I'm just going to take her to the nursery,' Isla said to Karina, the mother. 'She's looking a bit pale and the light is better there…' She would have loved to speak with the mother some more but the little girl was causing Isla too much concern and she moved swiftly through the unit, glad when she saw Emily there, who instantly saw Isla's concern.

'I'll page Alessi,' Emily said as Isla suctioned the infant and started to deliver oxygen.

Yes, Isla was calm and did everything right but there was this horrible new urgency there as Karina arrived in the nursery, tears streaming down her face.

'She was fine!' Karina was saying, and Isla could hear the fear, the love, the helplessness in her voice. 'Please, help her,' she begged as Alessi dashed in and took over.

'She's going to be fine…'

Alessi's calm voice caught even Isla by surprise. 'Just a little milk that's gone down the wrong way…' He was rubbing the baby's back and gently suctioning her, and thankfully she was pinking up.

He dealt with it all very calmly, even though there was some marked concern, which he explained in more detail a little while later after some tests had been done.

'As I said…' Alessi pulled up the X-ray on his computer and went through it with the mum. 'She has inhaled some milk and we're going to be looking for infection, which is why I'm going to have her moved to NICU to keep a closer eye on her for a few days…'

It had all been dealt with well yet it left Isla more shaken than it would usually, not that she showed it.

'Thanks for that.' Isla gave him a tight smile

as his team went off to NICU with their latest recruit and she headed into her office, just wanting to be alone, but Alessi followed.

'Shouldn't you be with the baby?'

'She's fine,' Alessi said. 'Are you?'

'I just got a fright,' Isla admitted. 'I'd just popped in to chat with Karina…'

'It happens. I want to take a closer look at her palate when I'm up there. I think she might have a small cleft that's been missed.'

Isla just looked at him and tried to fathom that in a few months she'd be on this roller-coaster.

'I'll try and call you tonight,' Alessi said, and gave her a light kiss on her lips. Isla wanted to grab his shoulders and cling to him; she wanted some of his ease and strength to somehow transfer to her, but instead she stood there and watched him leave.

She knew she had to tell him.

Just not yet.

She wouldn't say anything until she could tell him without breaking down, till she'd somehow got her head around the fact that she'd soon be a first-time mother herself.

It was just all too much to take in, let alone share with Alessi, when she didn't know how he'd react.

Which meant that at nine on Friday evening, after a hellish week at work, as Alessi drove home he called Isla and got her cool voice when he needed warmth.

He got distance when he needed to be closer.

'Is it too late to come over?' he asked.

'Well, it is a bit,' she said. 'I'm pretty tired.'

'Sure.' Alessi forced down his irritation. He could sleep for a whole week yet he still wanted to see her. 'Isla, I was thinking about tomorrow…' He was just so glad the weekend was finally here.

He had it planned.

He was way past the flowers and dinner stage already.

'How about I pick you up around six—'

'I actually wanted to talk about that,' Isla broke in. 'I've just realised that I can't make it.'

'You can't make it?'

'I forgot when you said you'd swapped your shift that I already had plans for this weekend…'

'Such as?'

Such as trying to get my head around the fact that I'm pregnant, Isla wanted to scream. *Such as trying to tell you that I wasn't on the Pill. That you were my first…*

She was closer to tears than she wanted to be.

'Alessi…' She swallowed. 'I just can't make it.'

'Don't do this, Isla,' he warned. 'I'm coming now and you are going to talk to me.'

'There's nothing to talk about.'

'You know, you're right,' he said, his temper bubbling to the surface. 'Because it seems to me I'm the one who does the talking. I've told you so much these past weeks, Isla, and you've told me precisely nothing.'

'That's not true.'

'Bull!' Alessi shouted. 'I know little more

about you than I did the night of the ball. You tell me nothing about how you feel or what you're thinking. Oh, sorry, I do know one thing that I didn't two weeks ago—you give good head.'

No, he could never know her, neither could he read her because instead of a shocked gasp or a swift attack he got the sound of dry laughter.

'You're right, you don't know me,' Isla said, because by her own silence he didn't and she'd surely left it too late to start opening up now.

'Game over, is it, Isla?' Alessi's voice was cool. 'At least have the guts to say it.'

'Game over,' Isla said, and hung up.

As Valentine's Days went, it was a pretty terrible one.

She woke to a text from Alessi, apologising, but telling her that she'd be getting flowers as he had been unable to cancel the flower order. And then there was a snarky addition: Believe me, Isla, I damn well tried!

Isla actually smiled wryly at his text.

She answered the door to her delivery of not one but two large bouquets.

One was from Alessi, saying that he couldn't wait for tonight.

The other was from Rupert, who must have forgotten to cancel his regular order from the florist.

'You have a very interesting life,' said Darcie, smiling.

Things had been just a touch awkward between them since Isla had found out she was pregnant but Darcie was nice enough not to push her to talk. Instead, she made Isla laugh as she swiped Rupert's bunch and said that she was going to pretend they were for her.

It was the only funny part of the day.

The only funny part of the week.

Isla's heart ached in a way that it never had before. She knew she had to tell Alessi, that somehow she had to face things—he would soon find out after all—but she was worried about his reaction. Of course she expected him to be upset.

In her work Isla was more than used to that. She knew, though, that after the dust settled, when the initial shock of a pregnancy wore off, rapid decisions were often made.

She had never wanted their fragile relationship to be put under such early pressure and, worse, it was her own fault. But on Wednesday night, as she set up for TMTB, Isla knew her problems were comparatively small as a very pale face came around the door, followed by a slender body that housed a growing bump.

'Come in, Ruby.' Isla smiled and she forced another one when Alessi followed her in with an empty incubator he had bought down from NICU for his talk with the girls.

He ignored her.

'I'm sorry I called you a stuck-up cow!' Ruby said.

'It's fine, Ruby. I know that I can be a stuck-up cow at times!' She gave the young girl a little hug. 'It's so good to see you here. Do you want to get something to eat?'

Ruby nodded and made her way over to the table, which was groaning under the weight of cupcakes Emily had just *happened* to have made.

Emily was always going beyond the call of duty and it dawned on Isla that she would be the perfect midwife for Ruby. Isla decided that she would have a word about Ruby with her favourite midwife tomorrow, or whenever Emily was next on.

And then, as she looked at the faces of her TMTB group, some nervous, some excited, others ready, Isla felt the first glimpse of calmness that she'd had since Darcie had pushed the pregnancy card towards her and she had found out that she'd be a mother.

She looked at Ruby and saw the fear in her eyes but also the fire. She looked at Harriet, who was facing things bravely and passing around a picture of the ultrasound.

Yes, she was twenty-eight but Isla forgave herself then because teenage, twenty, thirty or forty—when it first happened and you found out you were going to be a mum, it was an overwhelming feeling indeed.

She didn't feel so overwhelmed now.

Scared, yes, nervous, of course, but there was excitement there, too, and as she glanced over at Alessi, who was pointedly ignoring her, Isla was grateful, too, that, no matter what his reaction was, this man was the father of her child.

'It's great to see so many of you.' Isla kicked things off. They did a small catch-up, finding out where everyone was at, but when it was Ruby's turn she said little and Isla moved things on because clearly Ruby wasn't willing to share her news yet.

'Most of you met Alessi four weeks ago,' Isla introduced their guest speaker. 'He's a neonatologist here at the Victoria. A couple of you already know that your babies will be going to NICU when they're born. Some of you might not be expecting your baby to end up there and so, if it does, it will come as a huge shock. That's why Alessi is here,' Isla explained. 'If your baby is on NICU then at least you'll have a familiar face and, as well as that, he's a wonderful doctor.'

She gave him a smile but again Alessi completely blanked her and instead he addressed the group.

'Thank you for having me along tonight,' he said. 'As Isla said, I am a neonatologist. Does everyone here know what that means?' When no one answered he asked another question. 'Does everyone know what NICU stands for?'

A couple of the newer girls shook their heads and Alessi did smile now, but it was a tight one and, Isla knew, aimed at her.

It said, *Ruby was right—you are a stuck-up cow!*

'Well, a neonatologist is a doctor who takes care of newborns. In my case, I care for newborns that need, or might need, extra support. NICU stands for Neonatal Intensive Care Unit, which basically means it is a place for babies who need a lot of support. The best place for a baby to be is where it is now…' As Alessi talked,

Isla could see he already had the group eating out of his hand.

He was completely lovely with them.

'I'm very good at my job,' he said, 'but even with all the technology available, I'm still not as good as you are at keeping your baby oxygenated and nourished and its temperature stable...'

He opened up the incubator and turned on a few monitors and explained how they worked and what the staff were looking for, and really he did give an excellent talk.

'The nurses there are amazing,' Alessi said. 'When a baby is especially sick there is a nurse with them at all times, sometimes two. They don't get scared by the alarms, because they are very used to them. So although the alarms will make you feel anxious, don't think that the nursing staff are ignoring anything.'

Then his phone rang and Alessi rolled his eyes.

'That's my family ringing again and asking where I am,' he said, 'and that is one alarm that I *am* going to ignore!'

Isla smiled as he turned off his phone and gave the group his full attention.

He went through many things and then asked if anyone had questions, which they all did, even Ruby.

'What happens if a baby is disabled?' Ruby asked.

Isla had sat in on a meeting just that morning about her baby. There was talk of out-of-utero surgery, if a suitable doctor could be found, though Ruby didn't know about this yet.

She was in a very fragile place and Isla was very proud of her for asking questions.

'Many of the babies I look after will have disabilities,' Alessi said. 'When you say what happens…'

'Do you care as much about them?' Ruby asked. 'Or do you think the mother should have got rid of it? What happens if the baby is up for adoption?'

There was a long stretch of silence and Isla fought not to step in yet she glanced at Alessi and knew that she didn't have to. He was taking care with his answer as he looked at the hostile and very scared girl.

'The only thing I would think in that instance,' Alessi said, 'was that by the time the mother and baby get to be in my care, a lot of very difficult decisions have already been made and a lot of obstacles faced.'

He hesitated for a moment before continuing. 'A lot of my babies will leave the unit and require a lot of extra care just to do normal things. Many, too, leave healthy. My job, my goal, is to hand the baby to its carer, whoever that may be, in the best possible health. That is my goal every day when I go into work. You ask if I care as much. I care about every one of my patients. Some need more care than others and I see that they get it.'

She couldn't not tell him about the pregnancy. Isla had long known that but it was confirmed then.

She was keeping her baby and so the decisions

that would be made for its care would involve Alessi also.

She looked at his wide, lovely smile as he even managed to get a small laugh from Ruby, and Isla imagined his expression when she told him they were bound for ever—that the cool and together 'I've got this covered' Isla hadn't even been on the Pill.

She deserved his reaction, she expected the row, and she'd prefer that than Alessi choosing to do the right thing, to marry her, stick together…

'Now, I'm going to have to leave.' Alessi broke into her introspection. 'I have some time for some questions but it is my parents' fortieth anniversary tonight and I am already in trouble for being late.'

He didn't rush them through the questions, though. Ruby had no more but she took a generous helping of sandwiches with her and left, while a couple of girls hung around to speak with Alessi. 'I'll return this,' Isla offered, unplugging the incubator, knowing that Alessi had other places he needed to be.

She wheeled the incubator back up to NICU and chatted with the nurses there for a while.

'How's Elijah?' Isla asked.

'Well, it's still early days,' the senior nurse said. 'He gave us all a terrible time last week but he seems to be holding his own at the moment. Donna will be coming in soon to bring in some breast milk. She generally comes in at this time if you want to hang around.'

'Not tonight,' Isla said.

Tonight she needed to get her head around her decision—somehow she would tell Alessi, but away from here, Isla thought as she walked back down to MMU.

'Oh!' As Isla pushed open the door, there was Alessi.

Alone.

'I thought you had to get to your parents'...'

'They can wait,' Alessi said. 'This can't. I want

to know what happened, Isla. I want to know what's going on.'

Isla took a deep breath.

'Any time now, Isla,' he said. His phone was ringing and he saw that it was Allegra, no doubt demanding to know where he was.

'I'll be there as soon as I can!' Alessi had to keep himself from shouting and Isla screwed her eyes shut as he switched to Greek.

When he ended the call she met his eyes and it was time for the truth. 'I'm pregnant, Alessi.'

His reaction was nothing like she had expected. His face had already been pale, Isla realised, but it paled a little further and then he gave her a very small smile.

'Can you hold that thought?'

'Sorry?' Isla blinked.

'Allegra is at the party and doesn't want to make a fuss but she thinks she might be in labour.'

'Oh!'

'She sounds as if she's in labour.'

'Meaning?'

'One conversation, two contractions.'

'She needs to get here.'

'Try telling her that,' Alessi said, and handed her his phone. 'While *we* get *there*.'

CHAPTER FOURTEEN

IT WAS THE strangest car ride.

Isla's news hung between them while both were grateful for the pause.

Alessi wanted some time with his thoughts rather than say something he might later regret. *Is it mine?* was, for Alessi, the obvious question.

In turn, Isla was relieved that her secret was out and that the world was still turning.

'I think I've left it too late to get to hospital…' Allegra, from the echo Isla could hear, was in the bathroom.

'That's fine.' Isla's voice was calm. 'We're a couple of minutes away. I'm going to call for backup. Are you in the bathroom?'

'Yes.'

'Where's Steve?'

'Can I hang up on you and text him?' Allegra asked. 'I don't want the whole family piling in.'

'Give me his number,' Isla said. 'I'll text him from my phone, you just keep talking to me.'

'My waters just broke.'

'Okay,' Isla said. 'What colour is the fluid?' She heard Alessi let out a tense breath as it became obvious from the conversation that things were moving along rather rapidly.

'Clear.'

'Have a feel,' Isla instructed. 'There's no cord?'

'No. Isla, I want to push.'

'Try not push,' Isla said. 'We're at the traffic lights on the corner. Alessi's swearing because they're red.'

'I don't want my brother delivering me.'

'I know you don't want your brother to deliver you,' Isla said, and she caught a glimpse of Alessi's rigid profile. 'But luckily you've got me. I'm going to ring off and I'll see you in a moment.' She turned to Alessi. 'I'm jumping out when we get to the next lights.'

Their eyes met and there was so much unsaid. 'We're talking this out tonight, Isla,' Alessi said.

'I'm sorry, Alessi.' She told him the truth as the car moved the next five hundred meters. 'I wasn't on the Pill.' She felt his eyes on her briefly. 'I know I let you think I was… I meant to take care of it the next morning, get the morning-after pill, but I didn't…' Tears were threatening and she choked them down.

'Are you considering an abortion?' Alessi asked, and Isla shook her head.

'Then never apologise for your pregnancy again.'

She arrived at Geo's and walked in as calmly as she could, grateful she had been there before and that the staff let her straight upstairs as soon as she explained that Alessi was parking.

The speeches were going on as Isla made her way through the crowd and Alessi's father was speaking.

'Tonight I celebrate forty years with the love of my life. We have been together through good times and bad...' There was a long pause before he continued. 'We were blessed with three children, Geo, Alessandro and Allegra, tonight we sit in Geo's as a family, always.'

Alessi must have ditched the car because he was right behind her as she headed to the bathroom.

'Watch the door,' Isla said, and took a deep breath and stepped inside.

She'd delivered many women on the bathroom floor but she'd only deeply loved one of them.

Make that two, Isla thought as she stepped in and saw Allegra's red face and damp curls. Steve was there beside her and he blew out a breath of relief as Isla came over. 'Talk about timing,' Steve said.

'Perfect timing.' Isla smiled, dropping to her knees, knowing what to do.

'It's coming.'

Oh, it was.

'Get behind Allegra, Steve,' Isla said. 'Help pull her legs back.'

'Where's Alessi?' Steve asked.

'Gnawing on the door with his teeth.' Isla smiled.

'He must trust you,' Allegra said.

Alessi did.

But with no equipment, no help to hand, it tested Alessi on so many levels and it was a Herculean effort to stand outside.

Last time, with Niko, Allegra had nearly died.

It wasn't like last time, Alessi told himself.

Isla was there.

Isla was pregnant.

It was then that he properly acknowledged it. He looked at his parents, who were scanning the gathered crowd, waiting for their children to start speaking. A crowd was starting to gather where Alessi was playing doorman and a paramedic was climbing the stairs, wearing a crash helmet, which was possibly a giveaway.

'Yes,' Alessi said when his mother raced over. 'Allegra is having the baby.'

'Why aren't you in there?' Yolanda demanded.

'Isla's there. She'll call if she needs me.'

Alessi closed his eyes.

She just had called.

Private, deep, she had told him she was pregnant and he was eternally grateful for the drama of tonight, for not demanding to know if the baby was his, in some Neanderthal reaction.

Whatever the answer, he was there for her, too.

Alessi knew it.

Isla didn't.

'Is everything okay?' Steve asked, his eyes anxious.

'Everything,' Isla said, 'is perfect.'

Allegra pushed and when she couldn't push, she pushed some more and then let out a scream, not that anyone would hear outside, where there was music and chattering and laughter. And as Allegra rested her body against her husband, Isla demanded more from her.

'Again.'

'No.'

'One more, come on…'

'Do what Isla says.' Steve was both supportive and firm. Behind his wife, he held up her thighs and helped Allegra bring their child into the world.

Their baby was almost here—the head was out and with the next push it would be delivered. The door opened at that moment and Isla smiled as Aiden Harrison, a rapid-response paramedic who had arrived on motorbike, stepped quietly inside.

'Put your hands down, Allegra,' Isla said.

Allegra did and together she and Isla delivered the baby.

It was a gorgeous fat baby girl with big cheeks and chunky arms and legs, who cried on entering the world and was born with her eyes open. Allegra and Steve wept when they saw her, their strong, healthy baby, and so, too, did Isla.

Not a lot, but some tears did spill out, especially as Steve cut the cord.

'I think you've stopped the party.' Isla smiled

through her tears because the noise outside had faded.

'Steve...' Allegra said. 'Maybe you could let them know that everything is okay?' She glanced up from her beautiful daughter. 'And let Alessi in, poor guy.'

His face was as white as chalk but he smiled when he stepped in and saw his niece.

It was so completely different from the last time.

Then, it had needed to be all sterile equipment and everyone avoiding meeting his eyes. Then it had been his sister and nephew on different intensive care units and the joy of childbirth completely missing.

Now smiling faces greeted him and the surroundings didn't matter.

A backup ambulance had arrived and as Allegra was transferred to a stretcher it was Alessi who held the baby.

There were repercussions to his job. He generally dealt with the babies that had run into complications, with the battlers to survive, but this little girl was feisty, dark, hungry, angry… Alessi looked into very dark navy eyes that in a matter of weeks would be as black as his.

She needed no help from him, just love, and this little lady had it.

So, too, did Isla.

He loved her—of that he was completely sure.

CHAPTER FIFTEEN

A PROCESSION OF cars followed the ambulance to the hospital and once there a celebration ensued.

Isla was more than used to the excitement within a Greek family when a baby was born but it was all multiplied tonight, because this little lady had been born on her grandparents' fortieth wedding anniversary. Isla was aware, too, of the exhaustion having so many people around might cause for a new mum, but Alessi sorted it and suggested that the party continue back at his place.

'Thank you so much, Isla,' Allegra said as Isla went to go. 'It might not have been the ideal location but it really was the best birth.'

'It was wonderful.' Isla smiled. 'You made it look very easy.'

'It has been the best wedding anniversary present ever.' Yolanda was ecstatic. Niko was asleep on her shoulder and would be staying with his *yaya* tonight, but first they headed back to Alessi's, stopping for champagne on the way.

The mood was elated as corks popped and Alessi watched as Isla took a glass and pretended to take a sip so as not to draw attention to the fact she wasn't drinking.

'Are you okay?' he asked.

'Of course.' Isla smiled.

'Isla?' Alessi checked, because he could see that she was struggling.

'I'm a bit tired,' Isla admitted, which was the understatement of the year. She was exhausted. The high of the birth was fading and the enormity of her revelation was starting to make itself known. They hadn't had a chance to discuss it and from the way things were going it would be a good while yet till they could.

'Go and lie down,' Alessi suggested.

'I can't just go to bed in the middle of a party. My father would have kittens if I—'

'He's not here, though. Isla, you can do no wrong today, you just safely delivered Allegra's baby. I know they are a bit over the top but they really are so grateful and relieved.'

'I think it's lovely how happy they are,' Isla said.

He led her to the bedroom and she walked in, glad to escape from all the noise. Alessi closed the blinds and Isla undressed down to her underwear and slipped into bed. He came and sat on the edge.

'Thank you for tonight,' he said.

'I really didn't have to do much. Your niece made her entrance herself,' Isla said. 'She's such a gorgeous baby.'

'It will be you soon,' Alessi said, and watched as her eyes filled with tears. He could only guess how overwhelming this all must be for her. 'How long have you known?' he asked, and then answered his own question. 'The Monday before Valentine's Day.'

'How do you know?'

'Your texts went from ten lines to two words,' Alessi said. 'Don't worry about all that now. Just get some rest.'

'You're not cross.'

'Cross?' Alessi checked. 'Did you expect me to be cross?'

'I didn't know what to expect.'

'I only get cross when you dump me for no good reason, Isla,' he said. 'Get some sleep. We'll talk later.'

There was a lot to talk about but when Alessi finally got to bed around two, he certainly wasn't about to wake her for The Talk. He had never intended to wake her at all, but Alessi hadn't forgotten how nice it was to have her in his bed and he had missed her so much.

Asleep, Isla wriggled towards the source of warmth. Her back was to him and, deprived of his touch for ten days now, her body knew who it wanted and her bottom nudged into his groin and sank into his caress as his arm came over her.

Alessi lay there. No, it would be completely inappropriate, he told himself, because there was that damn talk to have. Except his fingers didn't care about such matters and were stroking her through the silk of her bra and then burrowing in.

'Isla…' Alessi said, which wasn't much of a conversation. His mouth was on her shoulder, tasting her skin again and then moving up to her neck. The response in her had him harden further, the craning of her neck to meet his mouth, the consent, the want had a flare of possession rise in Alessi and there was no conversation to be had.

Isla was his.

His mouth suckled her neck and Isla bit down on her bottom lip as he deliciously bruised her. His hand was sliding down her panties and she wanted to turn but she didn't. She liked the arm holding her down and Alessi's precision as he took her from behind.

Of all his responses, of all the reactions she had anticipated, this hadn't been one of them. Alessi's hand was on her stomach, gently pressing her back into him, and Isla, who had never been taken like this, writhed in pleasure as his hand moved down and stroked her intimately.

'Alessi…' She said his name, the only thing now on her mind as he moved her towards orgasm.

And for Alessi, here in the darkness of his bedroom, yes, there were questions, but her body's response, their absolute connection meant the only truth that actually mattered was easily said. 'I love you.'

Isla stilled, but Alessi didn't. He thrust into her and didn't let her get her breath, neither did he allow the panic that suddenly built in her to settle. He just said it again, for their love was no accident.

She could feel him building to come, feel all

the passion about to be unleashed, and it tipped Isla into raw honesty when she'd spent her whole life covering lies. 'I love you, too.'

Isla came before him and she loved how he held her down and didn't kiss her, or stifle her shout. He just let her be and drove her ever higher as he came deep inside her.

And still there was no need for The Talk because they had said what mattered.

Doubts belonged to the morning. There were none in his arms.

CHAPTER SIXTEEN

ALESSI WOKE BEFORE Isla and would have watched her sleeping had he not been so hungry.

Neither had had dinner, he remembered.

He wondered if she was as starving as he was.

If Isla was feeling sick in the mornings.

He just stared at her and wondered, which he'd been doing for more than a year, Alessi thought with a smile as he climbed from bed and went to the kitchen.

Coffee on, he started making breakfast and completely out of habit he checked his emails and then glanced at the news.

And then did a double take.

Yes, again she had him wondering.

'Morning, Isla…'

It was incredibly nice to be woken with coffee and breakfast and Alessi's smile, and she returned it but even as she stretched, doubts started piling in.

God, she'd told him she loved him.

Isla let out a breath.

Yes, he'd said he loved her but she was petrified of forcing his hand, thinking that Alessi might be simply making the best of a bad deal.

'This looks lovely,' she said, her hand shaking a touch as she took the coffee from the tray, unable to meet his eyes.

'Is there something you need to tell me?' Alessi said.

'Isn't what I told you last night enough to be going on with?' Isla said. 'I know it's a shock. I know it's too soon...'

'It doesn't feel too soon,' he said. 'We're not teenagers, Isla.'

'I know, but even so...'

'It was a shock last night,' Alessi admitted, 'but it's a nice surprise now. How do you feel about it?'

'Nervous,' Isla admitted. 'I was terrified at first but now…' she looked at him '…it's starting to feel like a nice surprise, too, but I'm terrified of the pressure it might put on us.'

'Like marriage?'

Isla nodded.

'You don't want to get married?' Alessi asked. 'Isla, help me here, because the last woman I asked to marry me…' She could see him struggling. 'I don't want to put the same pressure on you. Looking back, I can see that we were far too young and not in love. You've heard the saying "Marry in haste, repent at leisure". I'm quite sure now that that would have been Talia and I.'

'I don't want it to be us.'

'It won't be,' Alessi assured her. 'Just so long as we are always honest with each other.'

'I feel like I've forced things…'

'Isla, I was going to ask you to marry me on Valentine's night. I had it all planned, right down to if you said yes, we were going to go the next day to the restaurant, upstairs this time, and tell my family…' He could see the disbelief in her eyes. He rolled his eyes and then climbed out of bed and went to a drawer, and Isla watched as he took out a small box.

'There.' He handed it to her. 'Do you believe me now?'

She looked up at him and then back to the ring. It was white gold, with a pale sapphire. 'It matches your eyes, almost exactly,' Alessi said. 'I wanted a diamond but when I saw this…'

Again he asked a question. 'Is there something you need to tell me?'

'Such as?'

Alessi took a breath. 'Maybe there's something I need to tell you. I'm sorry if it comes as a shock. Your ex-boyfriend just came out. It's all over the news…' He saw the tears in her eyes and misread them. 'I'm sorry. Is this news to you?'

'I've always known.' Isla took a breath. 'There's never been anything sexual between us.'

'I don't understand.' Alessi frowned. 'Were you covering for him?'

'Yes,' Isla said, 'but he was covering for me, too.' It was the biggest confession of her life and far harder to admit than her pregnancy. 'I've never had a sexual relationship with anyone. Till you.'

'You're telling me that our night together was your first?' He shook his head, not so much in disbelief but that night he had felt her burn in his arms, the sex between them had been so good, so natural. 'You should have told me,' he said. 'You must have been so nervous…'

'No,' she refuted. 'I was always scared before, I wasn't that night.'

'Scared of what, Isla?'

'I don't really know,' she admitted. 'I thought I was scared of getting pregnant but I don't feel scared. Something happened when I was twelve…' She closed her eyes. 'I can't tell you.'

'I think you have to.'

'I can't tell you because it's not my secret to share, it didn't happen to me.'

'Whatever happened affected you, though,'

Alessi said. 'What would you tell one of your patients?'

'To talk to someone.'

'So talk to me.'

'My sister.' Isla gulped in a breath as panic hit. 'Please, never say…'

'I would never do that.'

That much she knew.

'When I was twelve I heard her…' Isla let out a breath. 'She had a baby, I think it was about eighteen weeks…'

'You think?'

'I didn't know at the time,' Isla said. 'I delivered him. Isabel begged me not to say anything but I got our housekeeper, Evie. She took us to a hospital… It was all dealt with, our parents never found out…I promised never to tell.'

'You're not telling me about Isabel,' Alessi said. 'I don't need the details about her, I need to know what happened to you and what you went through.'

And so she told him, and Alessi watched as

the supremely confident, always cool Isla simply collapsed in tears as she released the weight of her secret.

He held her as she spoke and then, as the tears subsided, Isla lay there and looked up at him and found out how it felt not to be alone.

'No more secrets,' Alessi said.

'I know.'

'You could have told me…' And then he stopped. 'I guess you had to trust me.'

'I should have told you that night,' Isla said, 'because I trusted you then, Alessi, or I wouldn't have slept with you…' She looked at the smile on his face and frowned. 'What's funny?'

'Not funny,' Alessi said. 'I guess that means that the baby's mine.'

'Of course—' Isla started, and then halted. Of course he would have had doubts, he would have been doing the frantic maths. Not once had it entered her head that he might wonder if the baby was his, but of course it must have been there for him. 'You loved me, even when you didn't know that the baby was yours…'

'Isla, I love you, full stop. We'd have worked it out, whoever the father was.'

He loved her. Isla accepted it then.

'Marry me?' Alessi said.

'Try and stop me.' Isla smiled. 'Can we not tell anyone about the baby yet, though? I want to keep it to ourselves for a little while.'

'And me,' Alessi said.

'We've only being going out for a few weeks…'

'Oh, no,' Alessi said, and took her in his arms. 'I've been crazy about you since the night I first met you and I was right that night…' He gave her a slightly wicked smile of triumph. 'You *did* want me.'

'I did,' Isla said, blushing at the memory. 'God, I've wasted so much time.'

'I wouldn't change a thing about us, Isla. You know there is another saying, Isla, *"Ki'taxa vathia' mes sta ma'tia sou ke i'da to me'llon mas"*.'

'What does it mean?'

'It means I looked deep into your eyes and I saw our future. That was what happened on the night we first met and that is what is happening now. You are my future, Isla.'

'And you are mine.'

They had a past, they had the future and, Isla knew as Alessi kissed her, they were for ever together now.

* * * * *

Don't miss the next story in the fabulous
MIDWIVES ON-CALL *series*
MEANT-TO-BE FAMILY
By Marion Lennox
Available in October 2015!